'You're quite a

'It took longer tha
ended up getting ex

'And what,' Angela asked, 'was that?'

'Me.' Dominic laughed. 'That does sound a little arrogant, doesn't it? But when I say "me", I'm not referring to my humble self, but rather to my wealth and position—the wealth and position to which, as my wife, you now have access.'

Dear Reader

With the long summer evenings, what better way to relax than by reading a selection of stories which really take you away from it all? With four exciting contemporary romances, Mills & Boon will transport you to some of the most exotic locations in the world. Enjoy the luxury of those places you always wanted to visit...surely the perfect chance to dream of your ideal man! Look out for our summer packs in your local shops or contact our Reader Service and indulge yourself in the world of romance!

The Editor

Grace Green was born in Scotland and is a former teacher. In 1967 she and her marine engineer husband John emigrated to Canada where they raised their four children. Empty-nesters now, they are happily settled in West Vancouver in a house overlooking the ocean. Grace enjoys walking the sea wall, gardening, getting together with other writers...and watching her characters come to life, because she knows that once they do they will take over and write her stories for her.

Recent titles by the same author:

A WOMAN'S LOVE
SNOWDROPS FOR A BRIDE

LOVE'S DARK SHADOW

BY
GRACE GREEN

MILLS & BOON LIMITED
ETON HOUSE, 18-24 PARADISE ROAD
RICHMOND, SURREY TW9 1SR

For Gordon

*First published in Great Britain 1993
by Mills & Boon Limited*

© Grace Green 1993

*Australian copyright 1993
Philippine copyright 1993
This edition 1993*

ISBN 0 263 78078 3

*Set in Times Roman 10 on 10½ pt.
01-9307-61326 C*

Made and printed in Great Britain

CHAPTER ONE

DOMINIC ELLIOTT leaped up Hadleigh Hall's circular staircase three steps at a time, his eyes gleaming with anticipation.

Angela would be in bed, he knew, and asleep, since she wasn't expecting him till tomorrow.

But he would awaken her with a kiss.

And in addition to the kiss...

Reaching the moonlit landing, he patted the inner pocket of his leather jacket to reassure himself that the jeweller's box containing the ruby ring was still safely there. His sensual lips curved in a half-smile as he felt the box's velvet-covered outline.

With an arrogance born of long familiarity, he strode across the landing and continued along the dark corridor, not stopping till he reached the entrance to the Hyacinth Suite. There he paused briefly to rake his black hair into some kind of order with his fingers, and then, heart hammering, he turned the doorknob and pushed open the door.

As he'd expected, the reception area was in darkness, but, as he stepped forward, to his surprise he heard voices from the bedroom beyond. Angela's low-pitched, slightly husky tones... and, overlying them, the deeper tones of a man.

The man laughed.

Mike?

What the *devil* was his half-brother doing here, with Angela, in the small hours of the morning? Dominic's brain, already a little out of kilter because of jet lag, seemed to stop functioning as he stared blankly in front of him. The door was slightly ajar, allowing a sliver of

moonlight to slant through, making a long V on the blue
plush carpet——

'You really must go.' That was Angela's voice. 'You're
most awfully drunk!'

'Drunk on your beauty, my sweet. Drunk on the love-
liness of your breasts, the smoothness of your
skin——'

'Please leave now, darling. I'm feeling nervous tonight. If he should find out about us, there'll be——'

'Don't worry.' Mike's voice was thick with passion as
he interrupted. 'He'll never find out. You've played every
card right, and soon you'll have everything you want;
you'll be able to look around as far as you can see and
know the land all belongs to you.'

'Please go,' Angela whispered.

'I will.' The words were spoken with obvious reluctance. 'But before I do... just one last kiss.'

'But one will lead to two, and two will lead to——'

'Two, my sweet——' there was the unmistakable sound
of springs creaking '—will lead to this.'

'Oh... oh!'

As he heard Angela's ragged gasp, Dominic felt rage
rush up inside him with such force that he thought every
blood vessel in his body was going to explode. He took
two strides forward, but his feet got caught up in a tangle
of clothing on the floor. Hardly knowing what he was
doing, he scooped the things up, and stared at them as
the slanting moonlight from the bedroom illuminated
them—undies, mere scraps of ivory lace and silk... and
a dress. His gut twisted into a hard, gnarled knot as he
recognised the garment; it was the red dress Angela had
been wearing the night before he left, the summer-scented
night three weeks ago when they'd made love for the
first time, by the lake——

He crushed the garment with a convulsive movement
as he tried to contain the frenzied tumult of his emotions.

Think, man, think! he ordered himself wildly as he
struggled against a blinding urge to crash into the

bedroom. Go in there, and what will you accomplish? Don't do something you'll regret...

Remember what happened before.

A groan of anguish formed in his throat. But even as he tried to force back the long-buried memories struggling to resurrect themselves, inexorably and relentlessly they came to life again and hurtled like poisonous darts through his mind. They brought beads of sweat to his forehead, a shudder to his body... and a pounding indecision to his brain, a brain that was now being torn in two...

Go in there, one half of it screamed, go in there and kill him!

Get out of here, get out, get out! the other half shouted warningly, over and over and over—*remember what happened last time, last time, last time...*

Oh, God, which voice should he listen to, which voice should he obey——?

'Hey, *man*!' All of a sudden a third voice was in his ear, not one of his own voices but a different voice, an unfamiliar voice, a voice that had a North American twang. 'Waken up, man,' the voice said. 'We're here already.'

'*Here already*'? As Dominic heard the words, which seemed to come echoing from another world, he felt as if he was struggling to reach the surface of a bottomless, inky black pool, struggling, gasping, sweating. 'What...?'

'We're at the airport. It's four a.m., man. Get yourself in gear, or you're gonna miss your flight.'

Groggily, Dominic blinked his eyes open, and as he did he saw bright lights all around him, heard the booming sound of jets above, and reality hit him like the blast of a shot-gun. He wasn't in the Hyacinth Suite at his Norfolk home—he wasn't even in England. He was in the States. And he was in the back of a yellow cab, which was parked at the flight departure level of the John F. Kennedy airport... and from the front seat the driver who had driven him there was grinning round at him with a full set of uneven white teeth.

Swallowing to get rid of the stale taste in his mouth, Dominic mumbled something unintelligible before getting clumsily out of the cab. As he fumbled in his wallet, the driver hoisted his case on to the pavement.

'There ya go.'

Dominic grunted a, 'Thanks,' paying him and adding a generous tip.

The uneven teeth flashed again, and as Dominic grabbed the case and strode towards the entrance the driver called after him, 'Have a good day, man!'

'*Have a good day*'. Dominic swore tersely under his breath. A good day was what he certainly was *not* going to have. When he arrived back at Hadleigh Hall, Angela Fairfax was going to be there. Oh, he'd never have known it if Starr hadn't happened to mention it when she'd called him—Patsy certainly had kept mum about the whole thing. Knowing he was going to get out of the country, Patsy and Mike had apparently invited Angela to be their baby's godmother—and, knowing he would be out of the country, she had accepted their invitation, and was going to be spending the weekend of the christening—this weekend—at the Hall.

Dominic felt his head pounding with fury. The *gall* of the woman, taking advantage of his absence. Hadn't he warned her, that morning after he'd discovered she was having an affair with Mike, that it would be better in the circumstances—he didn't have to explain what he meant by that; he could see by the sudden deathly pallor of her face that she knew what he was referring to—if she never came back to Hadleigh Hall? He'd made it more than plain that he didn't ever want to set eyes on her again.

He'd decided there was nothing to be gained by telling his half-brother he'd found out about the affair. He was sure Patsy didn't know about it . . . just as he was sure that by ordering Angela to keep away he'd put an end to it.

But now she was going to come into their lives again. *Someone* had to stop her from causing trouble.

And he was the one who was going to do it.

It would, he acknowledged, give him a certain grim satisfaction to see the look of shock in her beautiful, lying grey eyes when she saw him turn up at the Hall, and it would also afford him a certain grim satisfaction to send her packing from the place a second . . . and final time.

'*Have a good day*'.

The cab driver's parting words drifted back into Dominic's mind, and his lips twisted cruelly. Yes, he decided as he lined up to check in for his flight, it was just possible that he might indeed have a *very* good day.

Angela was, after all, glad she had come.

She'd always trusted Patsy, yet, despite the other woman's assurances that Dominic would not be at Hadleigh Hall on the weekend of the christening, she'd been unable to shake a nagging feeling of foreboding during the journey north from Brockton, a feeling which had intensified tenfold as each small station had whizzed by. By the time she'd alighted from the train, she was drenched with nervous perspiration, convinced that on her arrival at the Hall she would find a furious Dominic waiting to confront her.

And when she'd caught her first glimpse of the magnificent turreted house she'd felt her stomach muscles clench convulsively. She'd fully expected to see Dominic's tall figure at the top of the front steps, blocking her way . . . his green eyes as cold and contemptuous as they'd been that day five years ago when he'd ordered her to leave and never to return.

Her fears, thank heavens, had been unfounded.

And now, as she lay on a *chaise-longue* by the kidney-shaped pool, her eyes closed and a glass of chilled lem-

onade dangling from one hand, she felt the last vestiges
of her tension drain away. Savouring the caress of the
sun on her bikini-clad body as she waited for Patsy to
return from feeding her baby, she found herself actually
beginning to doze off in the drowsy heat of the September
afternoon.

Such peace. Not a sound in the still air but the
humming of a bee in the tub of scented white nicotiana
near by, and the occasional lap of water against the side
of the pool...

Her eyelids drifted open as she heard another sound,
the purr of an approaching vehicle. The sound was followed a moment or two later by the crunch of tyres, the
slamming shut of a door, the echo of steps on the gravel
in front of the house.

Half asleep, she turned her head in the direction of
the forecourt but a nine-foot-high yew hedge restricted
her view. Probably a delivery man, she mused as she let
her eyelids drift down again; Patsy had said they'd be
alone all day as her husband Mike and her mother-in-
law Starr had gone to London to meet an old movie
friend of Starr's who was flying into Heathrow from
California and they weren't expected back till just before
dinner. The other guests who were to be at tomorrow's
christening weren't due to arrive at the estate till after
lunch next day.

And Dominic Elliott, she reflected with a bitter twist
of her lips, was not going to be among them—he was
many miles away... as Patsy had promised her he'd be!
She found her thoughts straying back to the phone call
which had come from her old school chum—out of the
blue—in the middle of August...

'I know you and I haven't seen each other for five
years,' the pretty brunette had said, after the prelim-
inary greetings, 'but you're still my best friend. I want
you to be my baby's godmother—Mike's all for it too—
and I just won't take no for an answer. Look, I don't
know what happened between you and Dominic—though

I know it must have been something pretty drastic to made you cut us all out of your life—but I can *promise* you my brother-in-law won't be here for the christening. He's in Kentucky. So you see, you have no excuse. The ceremony's going to be on the Sunday afternoon—a private one here in the house. I want you to come the day before, so we can have oodles of time together and I can catch up on all your news.'

At her end of the line, Angela had smiled wanly. No, Patsy wouldn't get to catch up on her news. What she had been doing with her life for the last five years had been, and would remain, a carefully guarded secret from Patsy. From all the Elliotts. She would make sure of that. She would *never* go to Hadleigh Hall again.

'I'm sorry, Patsy, I just can't make it——'

'Tommyrot!' Patsy's tone was vehement. 'Listen, Angela, I warn you—if you don't say you'll come, then I'm going to take the first train to Brockton and you'll find me on your doorstep at Hawthorne Cottage before the day's out. I should never have let you cut me off the way you did. What's the matter, for Pete's sake? You'd honestly think you had something to hide!'

Angela felt her mouth turn dry. 'Oh, Patsy, don't be silly. What could I have to hide? It's just that...I'm sorry...you really can't come here—I don't have my own place. I still live with my father—he's retired now—and well...he really likes his privacy.' She grimaced as she uttered the glib lie. 'He doesn't encourage me to have friends visit——'

'Sorry, love.' Patsy's voice was as ungiving as steel. 'The only way you can stop me coming down is for you to come here.'

Patsy wasn't joking. Angela knew her of old, knew that when she used that tone there was no point in arguing with her; her mind was made up.

Angela sank down on to the chair beside the telephone table as her legs began to wobble under her. Long, awkward moments ticked by as her thoughts whirled round and she struggled to come up with some way out. But there was none. Or if there was one, she couldn't see it. The last thing in the world that she wanted was for Patsy to come to Hawthorne Cottage...yet it seemed that the only way she could prevent that happening was for her to go to Hadleigh Hall. She felt a dull acceptance settle over her.

'All right, Patsy.' Somehow she managed to sound light and rueful. 'You win. Thanks so much—I consider it an honour...and I'm longing to see the baby.'

'You'll come on the Saturday morning?' Patsy's voice was high with excitement. 'Mike and my mother-in-law will be away all day, we can have the place to ourselves.'

'Yes, I'll come on the Saturday morning. I'll take the first train—the one I used to take.'

'And I still haven't learned to drive so I'll have a car meet you at the station, just as I used to!' Patsy laughed delightedly.

'Lovely. I'll look forward to seeing you.'

And she *had* been looking forward to seeing her. She had really missed Patsy—they had been friends for such a long time, ever since they'd met at boarding-school where she, Angela, had gone as a scholarship student. Patsy's widowed mother, Elizabeth Clifton, had taken a liking to her—had probably felt sorry for the rather shy child who had lost her mother just before she reached her teens. And, since Angela's father was in the merchant navy and found it difficult to find someone to look after Angela during the summer, he and Mrs Clifton had come to an arrangement whereby Angela spent the summer holidays at Blackwell Manor, the Clifton family home. The grounds bordered those of the Hadleigh estate, owned by the Elliott family.

Which was, of course, how she had met Dominic...

Angela felt a cool shiver slide over her skin, and realised that she was now in shadow. Had the sun gone behind a cloud?

But even as the question flitted through her head she heard a sardonic chuckle. A chuckle that was oh, so familiar. A chuckle that was immediately followed by a light, mocking, 'Well, if it isn't the angelic Angela!'

Angela's eyes flew open and she jerked herself up from her lolling position. Staring aghast at the tall figure standing between herself and the sun, she heard herself gasp, felt the tumbler slip from her fingers and smash with a little tinkle on the brick tiles of the patio. 'You!' she whispered. 'But—it's not possible! You can't be here——'

'I can't?' His face was in shadow, but Angela thought she saw his features twist in an ironic smile as he glanced down at himself. 'I appear to be, though, don't I? Would you . . . like to . . . touch me, just to make certain I'm not a ghost?' He took two steps closer, so that the fabric of his trousers brushed against Angela's toes.

Many times in the past five years she had envisaged meeting Dominic again, bumping into him somewhere, but she had invariably pictured herself looking her best in some fabulous outfit. And she had always imagined herself being poised, aloof, indifferent, with a mysterious smile curving her lips as she walked away from him . . . leaving him looking after her with an agonised expression as he realised too late what a mistake he'd made in jilting her. She had certainly never pictured it happening like this, with herself in a supine position, her long blonde hair damp from swimming, her face washed free of make-up, her figure adorned in nothing but a faded pink bikini, while he . . .

He was the epitome of male elegance in his dazzling white shirt and emerald silk tie, black trousers and shiny black shoes, his suit jacket slung arrogantly over his shoulder. She raised a hand to shield her gaze from the sun as she skimmed a look over his unruly dark hair, his boldly rugged, tanned features, his sensual lips now twisted in such an ugly, hateful way. His face was thinner than she remembered, his muscular body leaner, sexier, harder...

She slid her feet from the end of the *chaise-longue* so they were no longer close to his legs, and clasped her arms tightly around her knees. 'Patsy said you weren't coming to the christening,' she said coolly, 'that you were staying with friends in Kentucky and then going on to Ireland to buy some horses.'

'Where there's a will there's a way.' His voice was as cool as hers, cool and controlled.

'But she said Starr talked to you yesterday—she said you were still in the States.'

He made a curt, dismissive gesture with his right hand, a flicking gesture that was more expressive than any words. 'I decided at the last moment that I should be here this weekend. After all, tomorrow is a very important day for the Elliott family.'

'Yes,' Angela said stiffly. And when Dominic didn't respond she went on—knowing her nervousness was going to make her babble but unable to stop herself, 'What a pity your father didn't live to see it; it would have given him great pleasure. He always loved children. I didn't know till today that he'd passed away—it was such a shock——'

'Dom—my father—had a heart attack five years ago, just after Mike and Patsy returned from their honeymoon.'

'Yes, Patsy told me. I was so sorry to hear it. I always liked him.'

'He liked you too.' The words were pronounced in a tone that was a clever mixture of incredulity and derision, as if Dominic wanted her to know that he considered his father's judgement had been sadly lacking in this regard.

Angela decided that the best way to deal with his nastiness was to ignore it. 'We had a lot in common. We liked watching old movies, liked gardening...and, of course, we both enjoyed playing chess.'

'Ah, yes, you did have a lot in common, didn't you?' His tone was exaggerated, as if he didn't really believe what he was saying. 'I remember those games of chess,' he continued in a bland voice, 'when you were at Blackwell Manor for the holidays. Patsy used to bring you over of a summer evening, then she and Mike used to desert you and take off together, leaving you to entertain my father when Starr was busy with her friends...'

And she remembered too—remembered how her heart had thudded frighteningly in her breast any time Dominic had come into his father's study while she was there. And it had happened quite often. He'd be on his way out for a dinner engagement, dressed in an elegant dark suit, and his green eyes had always glittered with casual amusement as he'd glanced at the two of them, their heads bent over the chessboard. 'I'll bid you both good-night,' he'd say as he swept out again, shutting the door behind him.

'Arrogant young pup!' His father's voice had always been gruff, but always threaded with affection. 'Time he settled down. Time he produced an heir. As the elder son, he'll inherit the Hall, and before I die I'd like to see him married. He may never do so, of course, after having watched his mother walk out on our marriage... and on him.'

Patsy had told Angela years before that Dominic's parents had split up when Dominic was eight—apparently his mother had run off with another man. Dom, apparently, had been heartbroken——

'It was his greatest wish,' Dominic roughly interrupted her musings, 'that his name be carried on, that there always be a Dominic Elliott at Hadleigh Hall.' His voice tightened as he added, 'I'm sure Patsy will have filled you in on the implications——'

'Dominic!' Patsy's incredulous shriek filled the air as she ran across the lawn towards them, her baby in her arms. She was still in her powder-blue bikini, her short, curly brown hair dancing around her head. 'Oh, you darling man, you came home after all—how lovely!'

Dominic turned from Angela, and, tossing his jacket on to a lawn chair, opened his arms to welcome Patsy and infant in a warm embrace. Patsy's blue eyes shone as she proffered her child for inspection. 'There, isn't he adorable? See how he's grown since you've been away, Dominic!'

Angela felt her heart give a painful twist as she watched the tiny, blond-haired baby clutch his uncle's index finger, watched Dominic's features relax in a delighted smile as the infant stared curiously up at him.

'He has... and my God he's the spitting image of his old man!' Dominic tugged his finger teasingly, laughing as the child's grip tightened. 'Where *is* Mike, by the way? I stopped in at the *Hadleigh Herald* office as I passed through town—he usually spends Saturday afternoon there, doesn't he, shooting the breeze with the ed? But——'

'Oh, Mike and Starr have driven to London—they're going to pick up one of Starr's friends from her acting days—he's flying in from Hollywood for the christening. They won't be back till around six. They'll be so pleased to see you! But what on earth made you change your mind about coming home? I asked you in early August if you could be back from Kentucky in time, but you said there was a certain gelding coming up for sale this weekend and you just *had* to be at the auction——'

'There'll be other geldings,' Dominic said with a short laugh, 'but only this one opportunity to see my first nephew christened.' Closing the matter, he turned his attention to the baby again, and began making little clucking noises.

Looking down at Angela, Patsy seemed to remember for the first time that she had promised her friend that Dominic wouldn't be home this weekend. She screwed her face up in an anguished, apologetic grimace. I'm *sorry*, she mouthed, her eyes pleading for forgiveness.

Angela stood up. It was quite obvious that Dominic's arrival was as much a surprise to Patsy as it had been a shock to herself, and she gave her friend's arm an unobtrusive squeeze to let her know she wasn't blaming her for this unforeseen event. Patsy's relieved expression showed all too clearly that she appreciated Angela's understanding response, but just at that moment the baby began to cry, and quickly she looked down at him.

'There, there,' she said soothingly, rocking the child gently. 'Still hungry, are you, my pet? I'm afraid I interrupted his feed,' she grinned up at Dominic, 'when I saw your BMW coming along the drive. I'd best go back in now... Will you both excuse me? I won't be long. Come on, Michael, back to the nursery!'

'Michael?' Dominic's voice was edged with surprise. 'But I thought——'

'Damn.' Patsy's smile faded and she bit her lip. 'I can't help it,' she went on quietly. 'From the moment he was born, I thought of him as Michael, but of course he's going to be Dominic, after your father. I'm sorry if——'

'No problem, Patsy.' Dominic's voice was strained. 'I just thought you had somehow found a way out...'

Angela felt confused. A way out of...what? And why on earth was Patsy apologising to Dominic? Why should she feel she had to apologise for wanting to call her baby Dominic—or had she been apologising for slipping up and calling the baby Michael? Either way, it didn't make sense to Angela. And Dominic seemed upset. *Why*?

As she tried to come up with an answer, Dominic scooped his jacket from the chair. 'I'll just get my things from the car and put them up in my suite.'

'Oh.' Patsy's face, Angela noticed, had turned salmon-pink. With embarrassment? It certainly looked that way to Angela. 'Starr—er—changed the rooms around...

after you went to Kentucky. She—er—put our things, Mike's and mine, into your suite. The master suite.'

For the smallest fraction of a second, Dominic seemed taken aback. Then just as Angela thought she must have been imagining it he said levelly, 'So...where would you like me to go?'

'Starr thought... the Tower Suite?'

'The Tower Suite?' He shrugged. 'Fine.'

'That's settled, then.'

Undercurrents. Angela could feel them swirling around her, but she sensed they didn't involve her in any way. They were between Patsy and Dominic. And the source was a complete mystery to her. What on earth was going on?

As Patsy walked away across the lawn, Angela told herself that, whatever it was, it didn't concern her. Firmly, she pushed the whole thing out of her mind... and, at the same time, tried to push Dominic from her mind too. He was here, and she was stuck with that, but there was no reason why she should let herself react to his presence.

Turning her back on him, she began picking up the shards of glass from the tumbler she'd dropped. Fortunately it had shattered into only a few pieces, and it was easy to gather them up. With careful fingers, she wrapped them in one of the paper napkins lying on the patio table.

'You could have rung for a servant to do that.' Dominic's voice told her he was still there, behind her.

She turned to face him, not flinching as she looked up into his disturbing emerald gaze. 'I'm used to doing things by myself,' she said. 'Unlike you, I don't have servants.'

'You could have had——' the thickly lashed eyes mocked her as he spoke '—if you'd played your cards right.'

'*If you'd played your cards right*'. What could he mean by that? Only one thing, of course—if she had kept her

virginity and not surrendered to him on that summer
night by the lake, that night when she had surrendered
to his tender, passionate advances, he would eventually
have married her.

'You set high standards, Dominic.' She made her voice
light and flippant. 'I hope you've found a woman who
can meet them—a woman perfect enough to be your
wife.'

'My wife?' He looked down at her coldly. 'That's the
last thing I need in my life—a wife! Why should I tie
myself down to one woman? No, Angela, my sweet,
there's no need for a man to buy the cow when the milk
is free.'

How crude he was. She scarcely knew him, he had
changed so much... or was it that she had misjudged
him in the first place, seeing something in him that hadn't
been there?

'You're a taker, Dominic,' she said quietly. 'In the
end, you'll never find true happiness——'

'A taker?' He raised his eyebrows ironically... and,
after a moment, shrugged. 'Yes, I suppose I am. But I
only take what the other person wants to give. For
example——'

Angela's heart gave a great leap of alarm as he dropped
his jacket and gripped her by the upper arms. But even
as she twisted fruitlessly in an attempt to extricate herself
she felt a wave of heat ripple through her at his touch,
at his closeness. A smile twisted his mouth, but it wasn't
the smile she knew of old; it was a thin, knowing smile,
which didn't add even a spark of warmth to his cold
green eyes.

'For example,' his voice had become harsh, 'I can tell
that you still want me, and your delectably erotic little
body still arouses me, so I shall take what I want from
you.'

Before she could gasp out a protest, he clamped his
lips to hers. The kiss was not like the kisses they'd shared
before; it was cruel, and punishing, and abrupt. It lasted

long enough only for her mind to register the dry, hard
pressure of his mouth, the rough sandpaper abrasion of
his jaw against her delicate skin, and the earthy male
scent of him in her nostrils.

But before she could begin to react to his attack it was
over. He didn't push her from him, just released his grip
carelessly, with a contemptuous curl of his lip, as if she
were some prostitute he'd grabbed on a street corner.

She wiped her lips shakily with the back of her hand.
'Don't you ever do that again,' she whispered. 'Don't
you ever *touch* me again!'

His eyes raked her body coldly, as if seeing her smooth,
tanned flesh for the first time. He shrugged. 'I may—
or, again, I may not,' he said. 'You seem to have filled
out since I saw you last. There's a voluptuousness that
wasn't there before. A richness...' Insolently, he reached
out and, hooking an index finger through the metal ring
joining the two cups of her bikini-top together at the
front, flicked it. It stung her skin even as she pushed his
arm away with a resentful exclamation. 'You look more
of a...woman,' he went on, 'less of an...innocent. But
of course that doesn't surprise me. Our little interlude
by the lake left me in no doubt as to your voracious
sexual appetite. And while you're here——' his eyes glittered with a glacial green warning '—I'll see to it that
I'm the one who satisfies it. No one else. Do you understand me?'

Angela knew that if she tried to answer she might
reveal just how close to tears she was, and she would
not give him that satisfaction. Clenching her hands so
tightly that she felt her nails dig into her palms, she just
stared at him, and prayed she could retain her self-
control, at least till she was alone.

'Oh, Angie, baby, don't do that—don't look at me
like that...it doesn't work any more.' He shook his head,
his lips slanting in a scornful smile. 'Those eyes—those
smoky, kitten-grey eyes, so meltingly beautiful, so
sincere, so innocent—so tearful. I *know* what goes on

behind them, you see, in that calculating brain of yours, and now that I do you'll never fool me again. I shall always be one step ahead of you. You would do very well to remember that. I'll be watching you, my angel. Every single minute!'

With a self-satisfied smirk, he scooped up his jacket again, and, hooking it over his shoulder, strode across the lawn towards the house without a backward glance.

Angela hugged her arms around herself, feeling chilled despite the heat of the sun, as she watched him through her blurred gaze. Watched the man to whom she had once given her heart so completely, so adoringly. The man who had used her body and then had tossed her aside. The worst kind of man, the kind who took pleasure in defiling innocence, and, having defiled it, walked away.

The man she now hated.

Dominic Elliott.

Father of her four-year-old son.

CHAPTER TWO

'I'M REALLY *dreadfully* sorry, Angie.' Patsy sat down on the window-seat in Angela's bedroom, watching as the other woman walked in her slip across the carpeted floor to the wardrobe. 'You could have knocked me down with a feather when I saw Dominic's BMW coming up the drive.'

'It's all right, Patsy.' Angela opened the wardrobe door and slid a sleeveless blue-green dress from its hanger. 'He's here, and that's that. Tomorrow I shall leave earlier than planned, though—I'll get the afternoon train back to Brockton, instead of waiting for the evening one——'

'But Mummy wanted me to take you over to the Manor for dinner,' Patsy cried. 'She's really missed you, the past five years. Oh, *damn* Dominic! It's all his fault.'

'Don't blame Dominic, Patsy. It's only because he's so fond of you and Mike that he's here at all.' Angela wriggled into the dress and, after pulling up the back zip, fastened the narrow leather belt. 'I'm sure if he'd known I was going to be here wild horses couldn't have dragged him home.'

Patsy hesitated, and then asked quietly, 'Do you want to talk about it, whatever it was that happened between the two of you? It was such a ghastly disappointment to me when you broke up. I know you'd only been going out for a few weeks, but you seemed so truly right for each other.'

'Right for each other?' Angela moved to the dresser and, sitting down on the blue velvet padded stool in front of it, picked up her hairbrush. 'No, we weren't right for each other. Oh, I must admit I thought we were. But actually, in the things that are really important, we didn't

22

see eye to eye at all.' She pulled the brush through her wavy blonde hair with slow, absent movements, barely aware of what she was doing. 'Patsy,' her voice was troubled, 'you confided in me on your wedding morning that you and Mike had been ... sleeping together from the time you were engaged——'

Patsy's eyes twinkled. 'I remember. And I was hoping that in return you'd tell me what happened between you and Dominic when he took you out for dinner the night before he left on his New Zealand trip. But you didn't...'

'Did he change towards you—Mike, I mean—after you ... made love?'

The mischievous twinkle faded from Patsy's eyes, and she looked thoughtful. 'Yes,' she said after a moment, 'yes, he did change. He became more caring, more considerate. Treated me, actually, as if I'd suddenly become much more precious to him.' She frowned. 'Why, Angela?'

Angela laid down her brush and swivelled round on her stool so that she was facing her friend. 'Because Dominic changed,' she said, her voice threaded with pain, 'after we ... made love.'

'Oh, Angela—so you and Dominic did...'

'Yes, Patsy, we did.' Painful memories clouded Angela's grey eyes. 'After dinner that night, we went for a drive in the country and parked by a lake. It was almost unbearably hot and humid, and Dominic suggested we go for a swim in the dark to cool off. Afterwards, he dried me off with his shirt ... one thing led to another ... and in the end we made love. I had never been so happy in my life—and I thought he was happy too. I didn't see him again for three weeks, as he was abroad ... not till the morning of your wedding, actually. Anyway, to cut a boring little story short, when we did meet again he gave me the brush-off.'

'He *did*? But *why*?' Patsy flung her hands out incredulously. 'What reason did he give for——?'

'I slept with him.'

'*You slept with him*? *That* was his reason?'

Angela shrugged. 'He said he hadn't realised I was—what were his words?—"the kind of woman who slept around".'

'Slept around!' Outrage burned in Patsy's eyes. 'He takes your virginity and then accuses you of sleeping around? I don't believe it! Where does he get off——?'

Angela held out a palm to stop the tirade. 'Drop it, Patsy. It's all in the past. I was just curious to know how Mike had reacted. After all, they are brothers——'

'Half-brothers...'

Angela sighed. 'Yes, half-brothers.'

For a long moment neither of them spoke, and then Patsy said with a perplexed grimace, 'I'm astonished Dominic would have acted like that. It's so uncharacteristic. I've never known him to be anything other than a perfect gentleman——'

As she spoke, the grandfather clock at the top of the stairs started chiming the hour and she uttered an exasperated exclamation.

'Oh, Angela—I'm sorry—I'll have to go. The caterer's going to be here in a minute—he may even be here already! I'm going to have to spend some time with him, telling him how I want everything set up tomorrow. Do you mind being left alone for a bit?'

'Of course not. Is it all right if I use the phone? Long-distance, but I'll pay for the call.'

'No problem.' Patsy walked across the bedroom to the outer room, and Angela followed. When Patsy reached the door leading to the corridor, she paused, and turned round. 'Angie, I know it was hard for you to talk about what happened—but I do appreciate your confiding in me.'

Angela's smile was wan. 'You're a good friend, Patsy.'

'Oh, I could just box Dominic's ears!'

'Forget it. I have. All I want is never to have to see him again, after tomorrow.' She glanced at her watch. 'Hey, you'd better get going...'

Patsy grimaced. 'Yes, I'd better.' She gave Angela a tight hug, and said, 'See you downstairs in an hour—in the library? We'll have a drink before dinner. Mike and Starr should be back by then.'

'Lovely.'

After Patsy left, Angela wandered slowly across to the desk by the window. It *had* been hard telling Patsy what had happened between herself and Dominic, because it had brought back memories she had tried so desperately to bury, memories that still had the power to tear the scars off her heart so that the wounds were suddenly every bit as raw as on the day they were inflicted.

Dominic—well aware of her innocence—had been so gentle that night when he began kissing her and caressing her, but his very gentleness had been her undoing. His skilful touch had caused unfamiliar sensations to shudder through her, racking her slender body with an ecstasy so exquisite that she had moaned aloud—and each time she had moaned he had become more aroused, his lovemaking more fevered. His breath had been hot and moist on her naked breasts as he sucked her beaded nipples and flicked them with his tongue; his hand had been cool from the lake waters as he slid his palm down her quivering belly, his fingertips trespassing where no man's touch had been before, making her gasp, making her utter little animal sounds in her throat...

Oh, God... Angela felt her heart spiral despairingly, felt her blood pulse wilfully as memories of that night, memories of her wanton response to his caresses, tumbled into her head. He had aroused passions that had washed away all her inhibitions... and she in turn had kissed and caressed him, mindlessly, greedily, recklessly. She had felt her senses thrill as she explored his muscled body, felt her head become dizzy as she found his weaknesses. She had revelled in the havoc she could wreak on his self-control with her fingers, fingers that had quickly learned how to tease, and please, and thrill... and with her lips, lips that had just as quickly learned to——

Stop it!

With a shiver of revulsion, she wrenched her thoughts away from the past, away from that night that had brought her so much shame and sorrow. Impatiently, she picked up the phone, determined to put a halt to this journey into the past, and, as she did, her eyes wandered abstractedly to the courtyard below, where a white wrought-iron garden set presided over green lawn as smooth and plush as velvet. And as she pulled back the edge of the heavy curtain she saw a familiar figure come around the corner of the house.

Dominic.

She felt her heart give a thudding lurch. Not wanting to stare, but unable to drag her gaze away, she watched as he moved across the patch of lawn to the garden set. She thought she saw a bleakness in his face as he sat down on one of the chairs, and, despite her efforts at detachment, a little murmur of concern came from between her lips.

He couldn't possibly have heard her, yet, as the sound escaped her, he twisted his head around and looked up.

Angela dropped the curtain abruptly, and moved back out of sight. That was all she needed, she reflected bitterly, for him to know she had been watching him, for him to guess she was in any way concerned about him.

She didn't want to be concerned about him—she didn't even want to think about him. She wished she had the power to eradicate him totally from her mind.

But of course that was impossible. Was forever going to be impossible. Because though her son looked more like his uncle Mike than like his father, being blond rather than dark, every time he smiled his crooked, totally disarming smile—the Elliott smile—she was reminded of the Dominic she had once known. And there was no escape.

Abruptly, she lifted the receiver and dialled her home number. She had just noted in the back of her mind that her fingers were trembling, when she heard someone pick up the phone at the other end.

'Hawthorne Cottage. Graeme Fairfax speaking.'

Angela slumped against the wall, her tension lessening just a little as she heard the familiar deep voice on the other end of the line. 'It's me, Dad,' she said.

'Angela! How are you? Everything going well?'

'Angela blew out a sigh. 'Not really, Dad...'

'What the devil's up?'

'It's...Dominic.' Her voice was flat. 'He's here.'

There was a pause, and then her father said, 'That must have been a bit of a shock! Can you cope?'

'Yes, I think so.' Angela smiled wryly.

'You don't have to stay, you know. You can always come home.'

'I know, Dad. And there's nothing I'd like more. But I can't. Patsy's counting on me tomorrow...not for the world would I let her down.'

'I thought Elliott was in Kentucky?'

'He was—but he's here now, so I'm changing my plans. I'll be leaving right after the christening, catching the afternoon train. Tell Nicky I'll be home in time for tea.'

'Tell him yourself!' Her father chuckled.

'He's not off to bed yet?'

'Molly came over this afternoon and we took him to the park. He met up with one of his pals from his Thursday morning play school and had a grand time— too grand a time...he's still winding down! Just a sec.' Angela heard his voice, slightly muffled as he said, 'Here, you little rascal, come and talk to your mother.' And then, more clearly, 'Right, say hello.'

'Hi, Nicky,' Angela said, smiling. 'How's my boy?'

'Fine, thank you, Mummy. I'm in my pyjamas. I had a bath and Grandpa washed my hair.'

'Good for Grandpa——'

'Sharon dumped sand over me. I heard Molly tell Grandpa she was a precocious child. What's precocious?'

Despite her despondent mood, Angela found herself smiling. She'd never known anyone who asked so many questions—and this one she'd better answer carefully, as her words just might end up being relayed to Sharon's mother. 'Being precocious is... being like a flower that blooms early,' she said, and then went on quickly, before Nicky could question her further, 'Look, I've got to go now, but I should be home tomorrow in time for tea. OK?'

'Oh... OK. Bye. Here's Grandpa.'

'Angela?'

She chuckled. 'You'd better warn Molly to be more careful what she says around your grandson!'

'I already have,' he answered with a laugh. 'But you seem to have saved the day—I can hear him whispering to himself, "Sharon's a flower".'

'She doesn't sound like a flower—more like a weed! Anyway, Dad, I'd better hang up now. You've got my number, in case of emergencies?'

'Mmm, got it right here. Thanks for calling, love. And chin up—you'll be home this time tomorrow, and it'll all be behind you. By the way, how are you enjoying the lifestyle of the rich and famous?'

'I'm not knocking it, Dad. I could get used to this.' She heard her father's quick bark of laughter. He knew she was joking. Though she had, of course, enjoyed her holidays with Patsy at Blackwell Manor, she'd always been glad to return home—had always been glad to be back at Hawthorne Cottage, the little house where she'd been born and brought up. It was a simple home, but a happy one, chock-full of lovely memories.

'Play your cards right,' her father said teasingly, 'and you might have a castle of your own one day. The rich and famous will be out in full force tomorrow, I reckon.'

'Play your cards right'. Angel closed her eyes briefly as a shaft of pain sliced through her. Dominic's exact words, the words he'd used when he'd struck out at her by the pool earlier. Oh, she just had to stop thinking about him; she had to stop letting him get to her. And she mustn't let her father know just how upset she really was. 'Yes,' she said airily, 'that's what I'm aiming for. A castle of my own...or a country estate at the very least. Perhaps I can snag an earl at the christening!'

'That's my Angie.' Graeme chuckled. 'We'll look forward to seeing you tomorrow. We love you.'

'Love you too.'

Angela replaced the receiver, and, with a yearning sigh, wandered across the room. How she wished that she could at this moment be sitting with her father in the cosy living-room at Hawthorne Cottage, perhaps reading a story to Nicky before he went to bed...

She'd moved across to the window, without thinking, having forgotten for a moment that Dominic had been there when she'd looked out before. But even as she made to pull back again she saw that he was no longer sitting in the white chair. The courtyard was deserted. A gust of wind blew a few leaves through the air. Summer was almost over, she realised. Autumn would be here soon, and then winter. She'd need a new coat before the cold weather set in. She'd put it off last year, because money had been scarce, but now she had the job at the Oakland Garden Centre, and could see that, with a bit of luck, her financial problems would soon be over. The last bill would be paid——

A sound behind her made her swivel round. To her dismay, in the doorway was the figure she'd expected to see down in the courtyard. Dominic...

How long had he been there? Panic spilled through her as she wondered if he'd overheard her talking with Nicky, but almost immediately the panic receded as she saw the expression on his face. It was mocking, not at all the kind of look that would have been there if he'd heard her talking to a child.

But what had he heard, then?

'So——' he pushed open the door '—we've raised our aspirations a notch or two, have we?'

'What are you talking about?'

He walked into the room. 'We're looking to catch an earl, we're angling to live in a castle.'

'Oh...' Angela shook her head scornfully, and was about to try to explain how he'd misunderstood what he'd overheard, when she decided not to bother. What did it matter to her what he thought? 'Excuse me,' she said coolly, making to walk past him. 'I'm going to go for a walk before dinner.'

He caught her arm in a steely grip. 'Uh-uh. No walk. Mike and Starr have arrived. Starr sent me up to fetch you; she's anxious to see you after all these years.'

Angela wrenched her arm free. 'Will you stop man-handling me? All right, I'll come down...but I don't need you to escort me! You go on ahead. I want to...tidy my hair first...'

He side-stepped her and, closing the door, leaned back against it, his eyes regarding her with hard challenge. 'So tidy it; I'll wait.'

'There's no need for you to wait.' She felt anger rising inside her, but managed to sound calm. 'I can perfectly well find my way down to the library myself.'

He straightened, and rammed his hands into his pockets. 'We'll go down together, and we'll stay together. I thought I'd made myself clear on that p——'

'I don't *want* to——'

'Listen, lady.' His hands were suddenly out of his pockets and gripping her shoulders so tightly that she could feel his fingertips digging into her bones. 'I told you five years ago I never wanted to see you again. I warned you not to come back to the Hall—but since you're here, and I can't kick you out because this place no longer——'

He broke off sharply, and closed his eyes, a look of pain crossing his face. Angela knew she could break free of his grip at that moment, but her concern for him was stronger than her desire for freedom. What was wrong?

She had never seen such a look of misery on anyone's face. But, before she could murmur the impulsive words of sympathy rising to her lips, he opened his eyes, and, clenching his jaw determinedly, said, 'I can't kick you out because it would upset Patsy. And the last thing I want is to cause her any unhappiness. *Do you understand?*'

His blatant hostility totally eradicated her feelings of sympathy. 'Of course I understand!' she snapped.

'Then while you're at the Hall you're with me, whether you like it or not. I shall be your shadow. Where you go, I go. I won't let you be a moment alone, because, lady, you're nothing but trouble.'

Resentment and confusion jumbled in Angela's mind—a mind that also stung from his insulting insinuations. Insinuations she could only interpret one way— he believed she'd slept with him in an attempt to seduce her way into marriage.

Then let him think it! She cared nothing for his opinion of her... and, after tomorrow, she need never see him again——

She whirled away from him and sat down at her dressing-table with a stubborn tilt of her chin. Her stomach was churning but she was damned if she'd let him know the effect he was having on her. With a careless gesture, she lifted her brush, and began running it through the heavy blonde waves. Ignore him, she told herself fiercely; pretend he's not there.

It wasn't easy. Though she tried not to see him, there was no way she could avoid being aware of his dark figure looming in the mirror behind her own reflection.

She had never before been in a situation like this, though it was one she'd watched many times in movies— it was a situation fraught with intimacy. She felt her heartbeats quicken as she slid the brush through her lustrous hair, the strands crackling, but, even as her heartbeats quickened, the movements of her arm slowed. It was suddenly difficult to breathe, difficult to do anything but force herself not to look at the dark figure approaching her from behind ...

Move! she heard a voice inside her cry. Move!

She tossed down her brush, and, rising with a quick, fluid movement, she turned and faced him breathlessly.

'There,' she said, 'I'm ready.'

He raised his eyebrows sardonically. 'Haven't you forgotten something?'

'Forgotten ... ?'

He nodded towards the dresser-top, and as she followed his glance she saw her jewellery lying there ... the blue-green enamelled earrings and the matching necklace which she always wore with this particular dress.

With a jerky movement, she picked up the earrings and, despite uncooperative fingers which seemed to have become all thumbs, managed to put them on, but as she reached for the necklace he scooped it up.

'Allow me,' he said in a voice as smooth and soft as silk velvet.

Bristling with hostility, Angela stood absolutely still while he draped the necklace around her neck, somehow managing to remain motionless while he fastened the clasp at her nape. She could feel his fingertips brushing her skin, and the sensation sent a shiver through her. His touch aroused her, his male scent making her feel almost faint. Despite every effort to keep her body under control, she shivered again, and she heard him chuckle. It was an unpleasant sound, one that made the hair at her nape stand on end.

'Your shadow,' he murmured, brushing hard fingertips down the delicate line of her neck, 'that's what I intend to be.' He slid his palm down over her bare shoulder, skimming it down over her arm till he reached her wrist. Clamping his fingers around the delicately boned structure with as much delicacy as if it had been a steel cable, he pulled her against him.

'Now, let's go down to the library. And don't forget—even for a second—that I'm your escort. If you should do anything stupid, you will have me to reckon with.'

'And I warn you, you won't like the consequences.'

Despairingly, Angela walked with him from the room. How could she have thought that she would be able to ignore his effect on her? Just the grip of his hand around her wrist was causing her legs to feel as if they had turned to jelly, her stomach to feel as if it was whirling like a merry-go-round. Digging her teeth into the flesh of her lower lip so sharply that she wondered if she had drawn blood, she forced herself to keep from uttering the cry of protest gathering in her throat.

Cruelty of the kind Dominic apparently loved to inflict was often intensified when the victim showed signs of pain; that she knew, and therefore she would never let him know how wounded she was.

It would be a small satisfaction, but she knew it was the only satisfaction she was likely to get.

The sound of Starr's throaty voice, raised in amusement, followed by a burst of laughter from the others in the room, filtered to Angela's ears from the half-open library door as she and Dominic crossed the hall together.

The ex-actress was obviously in one of her entertaining moods; with a bit of luck, that should help distract everyone's notice from the hostile vibrations thrumming in the air between Dominic and herself.

'Let go of my *wrist*!' She jerked her hand emphatically in an attempt to free herself as he pushed the door open.

'Not on your life,' he responded, drawing her forward with him. 'And don't frown,' he added sarcastically, 'or you'll mar that beautiful brow.'

The library was a large room looking on to the garden, with comfortable leather sofas and roomy armchairs arranged around a massive burled walnut coffee-table. One wall was furnished with floor-to-ceiling bookcases, and

by a tall window was Dominic's Davenport-style desk.
On the opposite side of the room from the french doors
was a deep alcove, which had been transformed into a
bar. A counter ran parallel to the wall, mirror-lined
shelves held bottles of liquor and in front of the counter
were several high stools.

'Angela, my *dear*!' Starr was the first to notice them.
Detaching herself from the little group standing by the
hearth, she moved gracefully across the room, her
willowy figure elegant in a taupe cashmere twin-set and
a black and taupe herringbone tweed skirt. Before
Angela's first visit to the Hall, Patsy's mother had
warned her not to expect Starr to look or act like the
American movie star she'd once been; ever since she'd
married Dom Elliott, apparently, she'd been playing a
part—the part of a member of the British aristocracy.
As a result, Patsy and Angela had amused themselves
from time to time by spotting what they termed Starr's
'props'—the old Burberry she threw on when going for
a walk down to the stables, the antique Rolls she'd per-
suaded Dom to buy her on her fiftieth birthday—even
the upper-class English accent she'd adopted, which
slipped only very occasionally. Seeing her now, with her
twin-set and the inevitable pearls, it was obvious to
Angela that nothing had changed, and she found herself
smiling as the silver-haired woman reached out and took
her hands in a light clasp.

'How very *naughty* of you to stay away so long.' A
faint trace of Balmain's sophisticated Ivoire perfume
wafted to Angela's nostrils as Starr's lips brushed her
cheek. 'But how lovely to see you again.' She scrutinised
Angela with the luminous turquoise eyes that had in days
gone by seduced the hearts of fans world-wide. 'My,'
her tone held a mixture of respect and admiration, 'you
have turned into a beauty, haven't you?'

She turned and gestured to the only person in the room
Angela didn't recognise, a tall, stooped man with grey
hair and a long, bony face. 'Max, come here and meet

our little Angela,' she commanded. 'She used to play chess with Dom—and even beat him once in a while, much to his annoyance! Angela, dear, this is my old friend Maxwell Logan.'

Angela looked up into the elderly man's lined face as they shook hands, and immediately liked him. Though his eyes were drooping, like those of a sad dog, she saw kindliness in the brown depths. 'Maxwell Logan,' she said. 'The famous director. How exciting to meet you.'

'Well, thank *you*!' A smile curved Max's lips...and transformed his face. Angela found herself revising her first impressions of him; he was, she realised, an extremely attractive man. 'It's always a surprise to me,' he went on wryly, 'when someone of your generation has heard of me.'

'Angela's an expert on old movies, Max.' Dominic slid his arm up and down Angela's arm, in a seemingly casual fashion, as he spoke. 'They used to be quite an obsession with her, as I recall. Isn't that right, darling?'

'*Darling*'? Outrage exploded inside Angela with such force that it almost choked her. How dared he? But as she looked up at him, angry words trembling on her lips, she saw the look of arrogant, mocking challenge in his eyes, and, gathering together all the self-control of which she was capable, gave him a cool smile before directing her attention back to Max. 'I'm not quite as obsessed as I used to be,' she said, 'but I must admit I still find many of the older movies more fascinating than those produced today.'

'I *thought* I was going to like you,' Max chuckled, 'and now I know it.' As Angela raised questioning eyebrows, he added, 'You see, I've been hearing all about you from young Mike here—he sang your praises all the way from London.'

He turned towards Mike, who, along with Patsy, had moved across the room to join them. Angela greeted Mike with an affectionate smile—she had missed him almost as much as she'd missed Patsy. Tall, with thick,

straight blond hair and the disarming Elliott smile, he
had put on a few extra pounds in the last five years,
Angela noticed.

'It's so good to see you again, Mike.' As she spoke,
Angela made to lift her arms and embrace him, but, to
her astonishment, found it was impossible. Dominic had
tightened his seemingly casual grip, pulling her close,
and now her right arm was tucked inextricably against
him, and with his left hand he had trapped her elbow
in a grip that was like a vice.

'Wonderful to see you, too, Angela.' Mike grasped
her shoulders and gave her a hearty kiss, obviously quite
oblivious to the fact that Dominic had her so inexorably
imprisoned. Feeling her cheeks turning pink with annoyance, she noticed the puzzlement in Patsy's eyes. Her
friend, of course, knew now that Dominic had jilted her
five years ago, and must be wondering what in heaven's
name was going on.

And just what *was* going on? Angela couldn't believe
that when Dominic said he was going to be her shadow
he'd meant he was going to all but glue himself to her
side. They'd be a source of great amusement to the
others, she thought, if he kept her clamped to him like
this...

'Let's have a drink, now that we're all here!' Starr
trilled. 'Mike, dear, get behind the bar, and open a bottle
of wine.'

Mike? For a brief moment, Angela forgot her irri-
tation with Dominic. Surely, in this house, Dominic was
the host? But, even as the question surfaced in her mind,
she felt Dominic stiffen, saw Mike's good-natured face
flush, saw him glance hesitantly at Dominic.

Angela looked up at Dominic too, and, as she did,
saw him nod unobtrusively at Mike. 'It's all right,' the
nod seemed to say. 'Go ahead.'

Starr led Max gaily across the room, and, perching
on one of the high stools, invited him to sit beside her.

Patsy trailed over on her own, a look of unhappiness on her face, her eyes fixed worriedly on Mike.

What on earth was going on? Angela wondered. In all the years she'd come to the Hall in the past, she'd never before sensed any undercurrents. Dom and Starr, Dominic and Mike, had all got along well. So what in heaven's name was causing these uncomfortable undercurrents now——?

She suddenly became aware that Dominic was guiding her towards the bar—and became at the same time intensely conscious of the fact that he still had her trapped in his seemingly casual but nevertheless inescapable grip.

'You do like white wine, don't you?' he asked smoothly.

'Will you please let me go?' she muttered under her breath. 'Or do you intend that we should spend the evening imitating a pair of Siamese twins?'

He loosened his grip, and she pulled away sharply. 'Sit beside me,' he warned, under his breath. 'Or——'

There were seven stools in front of the bar. There were three free ones to the left, and a vacant one to the right, next to Patsy. With a defiant tilt of her head, Angela slipped past him and hopped up on the stool next to her friend. In the bar mirror, she caught a glimpse of Dominic's reflection, saw an expression of frustration cross his face fleetingly. But it disappeared in an instant, and Angela held her breath as, instead of taking one of the vacant stools at the other end of the bar, with an ironic smile he crossed to stand beside her. She swivelled her stool immediately, presenting him with her shoulder.

'What's going on?' Patsy murmured, her tone bewildered.

'Lord only knows——'

'I've never seen Dominic like this.' Patsy pushed a bowl of pistachio nuts across the bar counter to Angela. 'Have you two made up again?'

'Good heavens, no!'

'Then——'

'Your wine, ladies.' Mike's words interrupted whatever it was Patsy had been going to say, and, before she could continue, Starr cried out, 'A toast! What shall it be?'

'Oughtn't we to toast the baby?' Max suggested.

'No,' Starr was firm. 'We shall toast the baby after the christening, when all our friends are present, and when we announce the terms of Dom's——'

'Let's drink a toast to Angela's return, then!' Patsy's words, slightly shrill, interrupted Starr.

Surprised at the tension she could hear in her friend's voice, Angela turned to look at her, and was dismayed by the pallor in Patsy's face, the strange glitter in her eyes. She thought she heard a sound from Mike, and, when her gaze flicked to him, it was to see that he was staring at his wife with an agonised expression.

But before she could come up with an explanation she felt Dominic's arm go around her shoulders. Firmly. *Warningly*? He tightened his grip, and held up his glass.

'To Angela, then,' he said. 'And her return.'

'To Angela!' As everyone else raised their glasses and drank, Angela forced a smile to her lips. A smile that belied the chaotic thoughts churning inside her. She felt as if she'd walked into some sort of a play—a mystery, in which each person—except herself—knew his or her part.

Yet, strangely, she had an uneasy feeling that she was somehow involved.

But it wasn't possible. This was her first visit here in five years. Whatever was going on, whatever was driving this drama being played out before her, she couldn't have a part in it.

No, she wasn't a player, she decided. But she was certainly a spectator.

And though she tried to tell herself that it was none of her business and she didn't want to become involved anyway a small but very human part of her was curious.

Perhaps, before she left tomorrow, the answers to all the questions niggling at her would be answered.

CHAPTER THREE

'MAX was a wonderful director in his day.' Starr, seated beside her old friend on a cushioned bamboo sofa, patted his knee with a proprietorial gesture. 'But before he began directing he had several triumphs as a character actor. Of course——' she treated the others to one of her dazzling smiles '—that was long before your time. Those early Prima movies were destroyed in a studio fire years ago, so unfortunately you won't ever get to see them.'

After dinner, they had all moved to the solarium, which was situated on the south side of the house, and were now relaxing with a pot of delicious coffee served by Nelly, the elderly housekeeper. The heat of the day had lessened as dusk began to fall, but even now, through the open french doors, Angela could feel a warm breeze . . . a warm breeze that carried with it the beguiling scents of a summer evening. How she wished she could excuse herself and go walking in the grounds. It wasn't that she didn't like Starr, but the ex-actress always had to be the centre of attention, and after a while Angela found her a bit wearing.

With a little sigh, she turned her gaze to Max, who was now talking.

'Starr and I met when we made *Love's Dark Shadow* together,' he said. 'It was her first starring role, and I had a bit part as one of her lovers. It was a very dramatic movie—in fact, Starr and I both thought it rather *melodramatic*! Do you remember, honey, when we used to rehearse our love scene together—you had such a hard time trying to contain your giggles? The script was the most appalling I've ever read.'

39

'*Love's Dark Shadow*.' Mike grinned as he looked over at Angela. 'Isn't that the movie we——?'

'Mike, darling,' Starr interrupted—rather rudely, Angela thought, 'would you mind shutting the french doors? I'm finding it a bit draughty.'

How could she be finding it draughty, Angela wondered, sitting in a corner away from the door, and on such a warm evening? But even as the question flickered through her mind she realised this break in the conversation was a heaven-sent opportunity for her to make her move. Getting quickly to her feet, she said to Starr, 'I'll close the doors. I feel a bit headachy, actually. I think I'll go for a walk in the garden...'

'I was just thinking the same thing.' Mike leapt up eagerly. 'I'll come with you. Angela, do you remember when you and I——?'

'Sorry, old chap.' Dominic was now on his feet and had moved across to stand beside Angela before Mike could take even one step towards her. 'Angela and I have a bit of catching up to do.' He slanted a disarming smile in Mike's direction. 'Why don't you and Patsy join us in a little while? We'll be down by the pond.'

Starr obviously thought it a splendid idea. In fact, Angela was astonished, and rather bewildered, by the other woman's enthusiasm.

'Go,' Starr said, waving them away. 'The last thing Mike would want to do is play gooseberry. Right, darling?'

Strange, Angela thought curiously. Five years ago, when she and Dominic had started seeing each other, she had strongly sensed that Starr disapproved of her— or at least disapproved of her as a girlfriend for her stepson. In fact, Angela had suspected a couple of times that Starr hadn't passed on messages she'd left for Dominic...but she'd been ashamed of her suspicions, and had never voiced them to Dominic, because she was afraid he'd think she was trying to drive a wedge between himself and his stepmother. Now, Starr seemed to be encouraging them to renew their relationship. How very odd.

Mike had sat down again on the sofa beside Patsy, and, as he put an arm around his wife's shoulders, he winked at Dominic. 'Go ahead, big brother—but I want some time with Angela later. We have some catching up of our own to do! Enjoy your walk . . . and don't worry, Patsy and I'll leave you alone. We've had our share of romantic evenings down by the pond—and the last thing you and Angela will need is to be joined by a couple of old married fuddy-duddies like us!'

Dominic laughed, but Angela could manage only a faint smile, and, the moment he closed the french doors behind them, she turned on him.

'Will you cut this out?' she hissed. '*Leave me alone. I don't need your company and I certainly don't want it!*'

Dominic fell into step beside her as she began walking determinedly along the brick path that wound past the sundial. Blast him, she thought furiously, he had ruined her walk. She hadn't wanted to stride along like this; she had wanted to stroll quietly, savour the peace of the evening, enjoy the lovely fragrances scenting the soft air——

'Slow down!' He gripped her arm. 'You might as well be tearing along Oxford Street in the rush-hour—I thought you had a headache. This is no way to clear it.'

She halted and glared up at him. '*You're* my headache,' she snapped angrily. 'I'm trying to get away from *you*. That's the only thing that will make me feel better.'

'You'd rather be walking with Mike?' His voice had a silkiness that almost, but not quite, concealed the steely tones underneath.

'Yes,' she said, with a defiant tilt of her chin. 'Yes, I'd *much* rather be walking with Mike.'

'Talking about old times?' In the half-light, she could see the contemptuous curl of his upper lip.

'That's right,' she said curtly. 'Talking about old times, with an old friend.'

'You and I——' his hand snaked out and captured one of hers '—are old friends.' His fingers trapped hers cruelly. 'You and I...can talk about...old times.'

'No,' she said, tugging her hand free with a savage jerk. 'I don't think that would be a good idea. There are some things that are better left in the past.'

'Yet you would discuss the past with Mike?'

'Mike and I are still friends. You and I...' She lifted her shoulders in an abrupt, dismissive shrug; there was no need to finish. He knew as well as she that they were no longer friends.

'And Patsy?' His voice was harsh.

'What Patsy and I have is something that time can't change. We may not have seen each other for years but——'

'You have no conscience, have you?'

'Conscience?' He must, of course, be referring to her having cut off all lines of communication between herself and her friend. She felt resentment boil up inside her. 'You were the one who told me to stay away——'

'You mean if I hadn't you'd have kept coming here, to the Hall, pretending to be the innocent——'

'I *was* innocent——' Angela clenched her hands into fists '—till that night with you. And for that you were as much to blame as I was. Probably more, since you were so much older. You were thirty, and I had just turned eighteen——'

'If I was to blame——' his mouth twisted cynically '—it was only because I tapped something in you that you had kept suppressed till then. Who would have guessed that Patsy's shy, quiet friend was such a hot little number? You really had me fooled——'

'And you had me fooled too!' she flung back at him. 'I thought you really cared about me. Instead, I found the only person you cared about was yourself. I thought you were warm and compassionate, but I found out you were cold and——'

'Cold?' There was an ominous quietness in his voice. 'Oh, Angela, there are many adjectives to describe the way I felt about you, but cold is certainly not one of them! And you're wrong, too, when you say I never cared about you.' His laugh was grim. 'That was my biggest problem. I cared too much.'

'I find that hard to believe——'

'Believe it.' There was a bitter edge to his voice that hadn't been there a moment before. 'They say that love is blind—in my case, that certainly proved to be true.'

She found it distressing, listening to him talk this way. When he talked of having loved her, though she knew he must be lying, it only made the shards of her heart, which he had already broken, splinter into even smaller pieces.

'There's really nothing to be gained by going on with this conversation,' she said in a flat voice. 'I'm going back in now.' She turned to go, and, as she did, added wearily, 'I don't know what it is you want of me, Dominic, but——'

The rest of what she had been going to say was jolted from her mind as Dominic grasped her suddenly by the upper arms and twisted her round to face him. 'What I want of you? God knows—I don't know myself! But what I do know is that right at this moment all I want to do is——'

His words ended on a tormented groan as he pulled her up against him, but, even as Angela uttered a little sound of dismay, he drew her much closer, so that her breasts were crushed against his chest.

As if at a signal, the breeze rose suddenly, whirling dry leaves against her legs. She barely felt them. Dominic had framed her face with his hands, his touch rough yet tender, and as she opened her mouth to protest he claimed her parted lips in a kiss that had her head spinning, a kiss that tasted of golden wine and summer nights, sweet and heady and seductive. The air was alive with the scent of earth, and grass, and trees ... but the only scent of which she was aware was the musky, male scent of the man holding her. It threatened to destroy every last shred of her will to resist him.

But even as she felt her body yield against him, even as she felt her lips soften and accept, even as she drew the familiar, primeval scent of him into her nostrils, somewhere in her brain a desperate voice called out to her not to be foolish, not to be reckless.

And, with a supreme effort of will, she obeyed that distant, warning call.

With a guttural cry, she grabbed Dominic's powerful wrists with determined fingers and, wrenching his hands from her face, twisted her lips free from his kiss.

Her legs felt as if they were going to give way under her at any moment, but as she stepped back from him she lifted her chin and glared up at him challengingly.

The only sign that he was disturbed was his breathing—like her own, the pace was quick, the sound harsh. 'You asked what it was I want of you,' he said. 'That, my angel, is what I want of you. Your body. And you—if your yielding response was anything to go by— don't seem averse to giving me it!'

Angela was glad of the shadowy darkness. She knew her flushed cheeks, the agitated rise and fall of her breasts, would give her away. The fact that Dominic was obviously not in control of himself, as he always liked to be, gave an extra little boost to her confidence and poise.

'Pheromones,' she said, with a derisive laugh. 'That's all it was, Dominic. Nothing to excite yourself about.'

'*Pheromones*?' He glowered down at her. 'What the *hell* are you talking about?'

She could see the flicker of uncertainty in his eyes. It gave her a certain perverse pleasure to know that, for once, she had the upper hand. 'Pheromones? Oh, they're hormonal substances secreted by bees, and moths...and by people, too, researchers have discovered! One of mother nature's clever little tricks, to ensure the propagation of the species. Pheromones, Dominic, are the body scents, male and female, which turn the other sex on. And yours, as it happens, turn me on...as you just noticed. But it's no great problem. All one has to do is look at it from a scientific angle, and then it's easy to handle.'

'My God, Angela, and you call *me* cold——'

'Angela, where are you?' Patsy's voice, clear and loud, came floating down the garden on the warm breeze.

Angela thought she heard Dominic mutter a soft oath, but from her own point of view the interruption couldn't have been more welcome.

'Here, Patsy,' she called back. 'Just a minute...'

To Dominic, she said in a terse voice, 'I'm going in now, and for heaven's sake don't follow me. I've had about as much as I can take of you for one night.'

Swinging away from him angrily, she hurried back along the path towards the house, taking advantage of the few moments alone to try to calm herself, and to set her features in a casual, questioning mould.

Patsy was standing on the patio, beckoning to her to hurry.

'What's up?' Angela asked as she reached her.

'There's a phone call for you.'

A phone call. Angela felt her stomach muscles give a little twist. It could only be her father. No one else knew where she was; no one else had this number. Surely nothing could be wrong? Was it Nicky? Had he come down with something? It must be serious, for her father to have contacted her.

But even as the anxious thoughts raced through her head she gathered herself together and managed to give an outward appearance of calm. 'Did the caller give a name?'

'Mmm. Molly.'

'Oh, she's a friend of my father's. I wonder what she wants?' she added, her casual tone belying the increasing urgency of her heartbeats.

'Do you want to take the call in the library?' Patsy stood aside to let her pass. 'That'll give you some privacy.'

'Yes, please.'

Patsy ushered her into the library, and, after showing her the phone on one of the side-tables, said, 'I took the call in the solarium. I'll just go back there and hang up.'

'Thanks, Patsy.' Angela lifted the receiver, but waited till she heard the click as Patsy replaced the one in the solarium, before saying hurriedly, 'Molly, this is Angela. What's wrong? Is it Nicky?'

'Oh, hello, love. No, it's not Nicky. He's fine——'

'Oh, thank heavens. Then what...?'

'It's your dad.'

Somewhere in the pit of her stomach, Angela felt the already twisted muscles tighten into a hard knot. Her voice shook as she said, 'Dad? What's happened?'

'He's in hospital, love. He wasn't feeling at all well...pains in his chest...so I called an ambulance. He didn't want me to call you but I insisted. We're here at the hospital now, Nicky and I——'

'And Dad...how is he?'

'I don't know yet, love. I'm just waiting to see what the doctor says. They're going to do some X-rays, and——'

'Which hospital is he in?' Angela could feel herself starting to shiver.

'Brockton General.'

'I'll be there as soon as I can, Molly. How's Nicky?'

'Don't worry about him, love. He doesn't really know what's happening. He's dozed off—and he's warm; I got a blanket from one of the nurses——'

'All right, Molly. Oh, how can I thank you——?'

'Just get here as soon as you can.'

The receiver clattered off the handset as Angela tried to put it back. It swung to the floor, landing with a heavy thump on the carpet. Fumblingly, she replaced it, and then, sinking down on the nearest chair, she hid her face in her hands. What was she going to do? There were no train connections to Brockton at this time on a Saturday night, and she couldn't possibly afford a taxi all the way home.

She tried to surface from the shock that had stolen all logic from her brain. She just couldn't think. Why wouldn't her mind stop reeling round and round as if she was drunk——?

'What's wrong?'

Dominic's gruff voice broke into her whirling thoughts. She hadn't heard him come in. Perhaps he had knocked, but the sound hadn't registered with her.

She shook her head, unable to look up, not wanting him to see how distraught she was. But when he grasped her hands, drew them from her face, pulled her up beside him, she couldn't hide her tears.

'What the devil . . . ?'

She felt him brush back the damp hair from her brow. The gesture, awkwardly made, increased the tightness of her throat, making it hard to swallow.

'Look,' he said in a low voice, 'whatever it is, it can't be that bad . . .'

'It's my father,' her voice cracked as she spoke, 'he's had some kind of a turn. Maybe a heart attack. He's been rushed to hospital.'

'Which hospital?'

'Brockton. Brockton General . . .'

'Brockton—that's a good two-hour drive.' His voice was vague, as if he was speaking to himself. 'If we leave now, we could be there around midnight.'

'*If we leave now*'. He was offering to drive her there. It was out of the question! Angela felt panic rise up inside her. 'No,' she started desperately, 'I can't let you; you might——'

She choked back the words that had come close to spilling from her lips. *You might find out about Nicky.*

But he misinterpreted the reason for her protests. 'Don't worry,' he said in a self-derisive tone. 'I won't make another pass. Give me credit for some sensitivity. Now go and get your bag and coat. I'll explain everything to Patsy while you're upstairs.'

'Maybe Mike could drive m——'

'No!' he broke in roughly. 'Mike is... Mike is Max's host; he can't just up and leave. Look, I want to drive you there. Can't you accept my offer in the spirit in which it was given?'

Angela dug her teeth into her lip. What was she going to do? As an obviously impatient Dominic waited for her response, she found her thoughts darting this way and that, in an effort to solve her dilemma. But she knew that if she turned down his offer she had no other way of getting to the hospital. As for preventing his finding out about Nicky, she'd have to face the problem when she came to it. All she could concentrate on at the moment was the fact that her father was ill.

'All right,' she said in the end, in a low voice, 'thank you very much. I'll be ready in five minutes.'

As she looked up at him, something... some indefinable emotion... flickered in his eyes. There was compassion there, she was sure of it, but there was also something else. Was it concern? Regret? She wasn't sure. But whatever it was it sent some answering emotion spinning through her. For a fraction of a second, everything else was obliterated from her thoughts except herself and Dominic, and the memory of what had once been between them——

'I'll wait for you down here,' he said, his abruptly spoken words breaking the fleeting, fragile spell.

With an effort, Angela drew her gaze from him, and, taking in a trembling breath, hurried from the room.

It was raining when they reached the hospital.

On the journey, she and Dominic had spoken scarcely

half a dozen words to each other; he must have sensed that she was in no mood for conversation, and she was thankful that he left her to her own thoughts, anxious though those thoughts had been.

The Brockton town clock was striking the midnight hour as she ran up the wide front steps to the main entrance. Dominic had wanted to come in with her, but to her immense relief she had finally managed to convince him that there was no need, that she had a neighbour waiting inside.

'You must go home now,' she said steadily. 'And please apologise to Patsy again for me. I hate to let her down like this——'

'Don't worry about that,' he responded. 'Look, are you sure you don't want me to come in with you?'

'No.' Hurriedly, she'd shaken her head. 'I'll be all right now. Thanks so much...'

Without waiting any longer, she'd rushed towards the entrance, and, to her relief, when she was passing through the revolving doors, she'd seen the red lights of his car disappearing slowly through the exit gate.

'Graeme Fairfax,' she said breathlessly to the nurse as she reached the information desk, 'where can I find him?'

'Mr Fairfax.' The nurse pressed a few keys on the computer in front of her. 'He's in Two North. Take the elevator up. You'll find the nurses' station right in front of you. They'll give you all the information you need.'

As the lift doors glided open on the second floor, the first person Angela saw was Molly. She was standing in the hallway, to the right of the nurses' station, talking to a short, heavy-set doctor in a white coat. The lift bell pinged as it took off again, and Molly's eyes flickered in that direction. When she saw Angela hurrying towards her, she said something quickly to the doctor, and they both started walking towards her.

'How is he, Molly?' Angela returned the older woman's sympathetic hug. 'Is he going to be all right?'

'This is the doctor who's been attending him, love.' Molly gestured towards the white-coated figure, 'Dr Ansell, this is Angela Fairfax, Graeme's daughter.'

'Your father's feeling much better now.' Dark grey eyes scrutinised Angela. 'It was——'

'Indigestion, love.' Molly's laugh sounded forced. 'Dr Ansell thought he ought to stay the night, under observation, but you know your dad. He insists on going home.'

'May I see him?'

'He's still in the X-ray department——' the doctor glanced at his watch '—but he should be back in, say, fifteen minutes or so——'

'Dr Ansell, please report to the main office...'

As his name was announced over the Tannoy, the doctor smiled apologetically. 'I'm sorry, ladies, I have to run. Be sure to phone me if you have any questions.'

As he made off towards the lift, Angela felt reaction set in. 'I'm going to have to sit down for a minute,' she announced. 'My legs feel all funny and wobbly.'

Molly immediately grabbed her arm and led her to a chair. Sinking down, Angela put her head between her knees for a few moments, with Molly murmuring soothing words to her. When she raised her head, she felt a lot better, and her thoughts had begun to clear.

'Such a relief,' she murmured, 'that it's nothing serious. I've been so worried, ever since you called.' She looked around anxiously. 'Where's Nicky?'

'He's in the waiting-room over there——' Molly pointed towards a doorway beyond the nurses' station '—and he's sound asleep. I was just about to pop down the hall and get a cup of coffee from the machine, when the doc came along. I still fancy a cup—how about you, love?'

To Angela, it sounded like heaven. 'Would you, Molly? I could really do with one.'

'I'll be back in two shakes. Don't go away, love.'

Nicky was all right... and her father was all right. Relief flowed anew through Angela as she slumped in her chair, and, closing her eyes, she let her head fall back against the wall. And thank heavens she had managed to stop Dominic from coming into the hospital with her. It had been touch and go, a narrow escape——

'Angela...'

Her eyes flew open as she heard her name. Jerking her head away from the wall, she felt her heart leap up into her throat as she saw Dominic looking down at her.

'You forgot this.' He was holding out her handbag. 'Left it on the floor of the car. I didn't notice till I stopped at some traffic lights, saw the buckle glinting...'

Get him out of here!

The warning words shrieked inside Angela's brain. Lurching to her feet, she grabbed the bag from him. 'Thank you,' she said. 'Now don't let me keep you——'

'Hey, hold on. How's your father?'

'He's fine.' Angela could feel her heart slamming against her ribs. 'Just indigestion. No need to worry.'

'You must feel relieved about that.' He frowned. 'Have you phoned Patsy? We should probably let her know——'

'No,' Angela said. 'I haven't.'

He looked around. 'There's a phone over there. I'll give her a call. Where's your friend?' He frowned. 'I thought you said——?'

'She's gone down the hall to get us a coffee.'

'Coffee. Sounds good—I might just get myself a cup after I talk to Patsy. If your Dad's really OK, then perhaps you'll be able to come back with me tonight——'

'Oh, I couldn't leave him!' Angela stared at him in dismay. 'He'll be quite shaken——'

'Let's wait and see.'

He strode away from her, and as Angela watched him cross to the phone she felt her panic grow till she thought her heartbeats were going to choke her. What was she going to do? Why in heaven's name had she mentioned coffee? Was he intending to hang around? How could she get rid of him before——?

But even as the frantic questions swirled round her head she saw a small, forlorn-looking figure come out of the waiting-room beyond the nurses' station. Rubbing his eyes, Nicky didn't see her. He stumbled drowsily to the desk.

'Has my mummy come yet?' he asked.

Angela darted a desperate glance at Dominic, and saw that he was already talking on the phone. He must have got through right away. She clenched her fists. Every instinct screamed at her to run to Nicky, gather him up in her arms, get him away from this place before Dominic saw him...

But her legs wouldn't move.

Her senses, though, had become strangely, intensely acute. As if it were happening in slow motion, she watched the scene before her unfold. She saw Dominic put the phone down, saw him turn, saw him start walking towards her. She saw the nurse look in her direction, saw her raise her eyebrows questioningly and point at her, saw Nicky grin and give an enthusiastic nod.

'Good!' The nurse's voice was clear in the stillness. 'Your mummy's just been waiting for you to wake up. Off you go, pet.'

The scene was still unfolding in slow motion as Nicky started running towards her. He was wearing a pair of faded blue jeans and a red and cream striped sweatshirt. His straight blond hair was tousled and his face was pale, but his blue eyes were alight with happiness. His trainers made a light padding sound on the tiled floor.

'Mummy!' he cried as he threw his small sturdy figure at her, barely glancing at the man who had come to an abrupt halt a few feet away and was staring at him with a stunned expression on his face. 'You're back! I knew you'd come.'

CHAPTER FOUR

'THERE'S no denying who *his* father is!'

The words echoed in Angela's ears an hour later as she stood alone at her bedroom window overlooking the garden. The moon was full, its silvered beams reflected on the white-painted picket fence surrounding the cottage. She winced as she recalled the hostility in Dominic's eyes as he spoke the words in a tone that chilled her... an accusing tone that had confirmed to her, beyond a doubt, that he'd realised immediately that Nicky was his child.

They hadn't had an opportunity to talk at the hospital, because no sooner had Nicky flung himself at her than Molly had returned with the coffee, and behind her, being trundled along in a hospital wheelchair, was her father. He was ready to leave, and, when Molly had said she'd go and phone for a taxi, before Angela could protest Dominic had offered to drive everyone home.

Graeme had looked up sharply as this tall, dark stranger had proceeded to introduce himself. For a long moment, the two men had scrutinised each other, Dominic's penetrating green eyes steadily meeting the shrewd grey ones of Angela's father. She had stood with her hands tightly on Nicky's shoulders, her own gaze fixed on her father as the men sized each other up. Graeme Fairfax had always prided himself on being a good judge of character, and she waited with her breath caught in her throat, expecting him to turn down Dominic's offer curtly. Though she had never told her father what had caused the break-up of her relationship with Dominic, she'd always assumed that, having seen her intense unhappiness at that time and during the months following, he would have guessed it wasn't something she had wanted. Perhaps now he would give a piece of his mind to this man who had caused his daughter so much pain.

Instead, to her astonishment, he reached up a hand. 'Graeme Fairfax,' he said. 'Angela's dad. Pleased to meet you, Elliott... and pleased to accept your kind offer. That'll save us a few pennies, I reckon,' he went on with a grin. 'Angie, lass, lead the way and let's get out of here. Put the boy on my lap—he may as well get a free ride.'

Angela had sat in seething silence all the way home. They had dropped Molly off at her place, and then Dominic had parked in front of Hawthorne Cottage, before assisting her father up the path to the front door. Nicky had fallen asleep in the car, and Angela carried him in and put him straight to bed. Upon going through to the living-room, she discovered, to her dismay, that her father had invited Dominic to spend the night. Graeme had then gone to bed, leaving the two of them together.

And that was when Dominic had said to her, 'There's no denying who *his* father is!'

At Angela's defiantly retorted, 'I'm not *trying* to deny it,' he had demanded harshly,

'And what do you intend doing about it?'

'I intend to do nothing about it.' She was glad her voice was calm, revealing nothing of her inner turmoil. 'My decisions were all made a long time ago.' Made, in fact, at the time of Nicky's birth, when she'd decided that Dominic had no rights regarding his son. She had to admit that in the beginning she'd been persistently tormented by a little voice deep inside that had told her it was his right to know he had fathered a child... but in the end her bitterness had won out. 'Nicky is my son,' she went on, 'and I'm going——'

'His name's Nicky?'

'We call him Nicky... but he was baptised Dominic.' Angela tilted her chin defiantly as she saw the stunned look on Dominic's face. 'I called him after your father——'

'My *God*,' he blazed, 'you have some nerve! Did it never occur to you that——?'

'As I was saying,' Angela broke in and continued as if his violent interruption had never taken place, 'Nicky is my son and I'm going to bring him up myself.'

'It's out of the question, of course, for you to ever think of taking him to the Hall!'

'That's the last place I'd think of taking him,' she returned with a cold twist of her lips.

'Who knows about him?' Dominic stepped towards her, and she stepped back, sensing menace in his swift movement.

'Knows about him?' Her laugh was ironic. 'Hundreds of people. Our neighbours, his nursery school teachers, the check-out girls at the supermarket——'

'You know damned well that's not what I'm talking about,' he lashed out at her. 'How many people know who his father is?'

'Dad is the only person who knows——'

'Does Mike?'

'Mike?' Confused, Angela shook her head. 'No, he doesn't...of course he doesn't.'

'Thank God for that!'

'My father knows...I know...and now you know. And I want it to remain that way.'

'Good,' he said, ramming his hands roughly into his trouser pockets. 'I'm glad you at least have sense enough to realise the problems you could cause if you didn't.'

Yes, she could see it would raise problems...for him. He would be put in the position of having to explain to his family and friends why he had courted her, slept with her...and then deserted her.

'You have no reason to worry,' she said curtly. 'And now, if you'll excuse me, I'm going to bed. I wish my father hadn't invited you to stay over...but what's done is done, and it is, after all, his house. Just make sure you don't hang around in the morning.'

'I don't intend to. I think we should leave around ten.'

'*We*?' Surely he didn't think she was going to return to the Hall—had she known he was going to turn up there for the christening she'd never have gone there in the first place. Her father's emergency trip to the hospital had given her a heaven-sent opportunity to come home, and now that she was safely here, here was where she was going to stay. Only a fool would subject herself to the kind of treatment Dominic had been dishing out to her.

'Yes, we—you and I,' Dominic said with a trace of impatience. 'Your father told me he's going to have Molly come over and keep him company tomorrow, and give him a hand with your son. He wants you to attend the christening.'

'You must be *crazy* if you think I'd go back—and I can't for the life of me see why you would want me to. You've gone out of your way to make me feel unwelcome at——'

'For God's sake, think of somebody else but yourself for a change. If your father were seriously ill, Patsy would never expect you to come back. But in the circumstances...'

He didn't need to go on. As Angela imagined the disappointment on Patsy's face when she discovered that her old friend could have returned but chose not to do so, she realised, with a feeling of despair, that she had no choice.

'All right,' she said in a defeated tone. 'I'll go back with you. And now... I *am* going to bed.' She cleared her throat. 'Did Dad tell you where you'd be sleeping?'

'Oh, yes,' he said drily, 'Graeme told me where I'd be sleeping. In the room next to his—he told me he hoped I didn't snore because he can hear every sound through the wall. Do you think,' he asked with a sardonic lift of one eyebrow, 'that your father was trying to tell me something?'

'I should say he was trying to let you know he doesn't trust you,' Angela retorted.

'Or perhaps he was trying to tell me he doesn't trust *you*.'

'Hell will freeze over before I ever come to your bed, Dominic!'

And on that scathing note she'd made her exit.

She had thought she was tired, but, once in bed, she couldn't sleep, and had got up and prowled restlessly around her room. Now, standing by the window, she found her thoughts drifting again and again to Dominic. Hawthorne Cottage was so small, she could almost swear she heard him breathing, in the tiny room down the hall. She could imagine him lying on the single bed, his lean body spread out as he relaxed in sleep.

Hell would freeze over, she had said, before she'd ever come to his bed.

Yet as she stood there with the breeze ruffling the lace yoke of her lawn nightgown, fanning her warm cheeks, lifting light strands of her hair, she felt a traitorous, inexorable aching inside her... an aching to be close to him. To be lying in that bed with him. To be yielding to his lovemaking, to recapture the ecstasy they'd once shared, on that night by the lake that now seemed so very far away.

And the knowledge that she felt this way, about a man she should despise, filled her with shame... but that shame did nothing whatsoever to assuage the restless desire that was swimming like liquid fire in her blood.

'Good morning, Mummy!' Nicky poked his head round her bedroom door next morning just as she finished making her bed. 'Grandpa sent me up to tell you breakfast's ready. We're all waiting for you.'

'Thanks, Nicky.' Angela managed to produce a bright smile. 'I'll be right down.'

As Nicky's feet clattered away down the stairs, the smile faded away. *'We're all waiting for you'*. The *all*, of course, included Dominic. How disturbing it was, having him here at the cottage. In her home. Among the things that had been familiar to her all her life. There was an *intimacy* about it that set her nerves quivering. It was as if his presence, somehow, infiltrated the whole house...

But it wouldn't, thank heavens, be for much longer.

Resisting the compelling urge to check her reflection in the wardrobe mirror, she put on her slippers and crossed to the door, and, with her heartbeats fluttering as wildly as the wings of a drowning bird, she walked down the stairs and across the hall to the kitchen. There she paused for a moment in the doorway, and tried to steady her breathing.

Nicky was sitting at the table, and her father was at the stove, but it was to Dominic that her eyes traitorously flew... and as she let her gaze skim over him she found herself grasping the door-frame for support. He was at the counter-top by the window, filling three mugs with coffee, and she felt her legs turn weak as she looked at him. He was wearing the same white shirt he'd been wearing the day before—though the collar was still crisp, the fabric stretched over his wide shoulders was creased—and the same dark trousers, which sheathed his thighs in such a way that every hard muscle was defined. His jaw was unshaven, and his black hair looked as if it hadn't been combed in a week. How, she wondered despairingly, could a man who looked as if he'd slept in his clothes still be the picture of male elegance— rugged male elegance, granted, but male elegance nevertheless?

Her eyes followed the movement of his arm as he rubbed the back of one hand over his darkly bristled jaw, making a rasping sound that unexpectedly stimulated a strange aching deep inside her. How would it feel to caress that jaw? she found herself wondering dizzily.

How would it feel to have that sandpaper-rough skin brush her own delicate skin——?

She dragged her gaze away and cleared her throat. 'Morning, Dad,' she said. 'How are you feeling today?'

Her father looked round. 'Ah, good morning, lass. How do I feel?' He grinned. 'Never better.'

Out of the corner of her eye, Angela saw Dominic put down the coffee-pot, saw him move to the table and draw out a chair for her. 'Good morning, Angela,' he said lazily. 'Did you sleep well?'

For just a second his pleasant tone threw her, and then she realised that he was putting on an act for her father's sake—and, for her father's sake, she decided to go along with it.

'Good morning, Dominic. Yes, thank you, I slept well.' Her tone was as pleasant as his, but as she spoke her cheeks turned warm. He was giving her the once-over, just as she had done to him moments before. His gaze roamed over her body with an arrogance that fired a flame of anger inside her, his sensual lips twitching in a taunting smile as he took in every detail of her appearance, from the lustrous sweep of her long blonde hair to the raspberry lipstick adorning her full lips, to the subtly applied silver-grey eyeshadow and the hint of blush. Thank heavens she had worn her loose-fitting red sweatshirt, she thought; at least her curves were well concealed.

Sitting down, she made sure she didn't touch him, but as he pushed in her chair he brushed his fingers against her nape. On purpose, she knew. Electricity sparked between them, making her jump.

'Stop that,' she hissed under her breath.

His mouth widened in a fake smile. 'Sorry,' he said with exaggerated penitence.

Her father seemed quite oblivious to the hostility sizzling between them, as he carried a platter of bacon and eggs to the table and sat down. 'I'm the housekeeper here, Elliott,' he remarked as Dominic brought the mugs of coffee to the table. 'Have been for over four years now. I retired about eleven months after Nicky was born, and since it was time for Angela to get herself some training it seemed natural for me to take over the house. Always enjoyed keeping a tidy ship—used to be in the merchant navy.'

'Must have been a fascinating life, aboard ship.' Dominic pulled back his chair and sat down as Graeme dished out the bacon and eggs.

Angela saw her father's face light up; there was nothing he liked better than reminiscing about his sea-going days, and Dominic's words were all the invitation he needed. Keeping her eyes fixed on her plate, she chewed her way through her bacon and eggs, and, though she usually enjoyed her Sunday breakfast, today she might as well have been chewing wet rope. Her father's voice flowed over her, his old stories so familiar to her that she could have told them all herself. As she finally swallowed the last mouthful of her breakfast, she darted a quick glance at Dominic from under her lashes, and felt her heartbeats stumble. He was looking not at her father but at Nicky—staring at his blond hair, which was thick and straight, like Mike's...and like Dom's too, before it had turned grey...and she felt a shiver run down her spine. He wasn't looking at the child in the curious, assessing way a man might look at his newly found son, but looking at him rather with an expression of profound sorrow...sorrow laced with pain. Angela felt a stab of alarm. Was he really regretting that after today he would never see his child again? Was he going to change his mind about that? Fighting down her rising panic, Angela turned to Nicky as he touched her arm.

'Mummy,' he whispered, 'I'm finished. May I leave the table? I want to go for a ride on my bike.'

Thankful of the excuse to get away from Dominic, if only temporarily, she said, 'Mmm. Just for five minutes. I'll come with you. Will you excuse me, Dad? I'm going to take Nicky out for a turn on his bike before we leave.'

'There's no rush, surely, lass? The christening isn't till the afternoon. Take the boy up the river. And take Dominic with you. Show him the swinging bridge.'

Before Angela could come up with some reason not to do as her father asked, Nicky grabbed one of Dominic's hands and tried to pull him to his feet. 'Come on, Dominic,' he cried. 'The swinging bridge is fun. Wait till you see it!'

Dominic sat there for a moment without answering, without moving, Nicky's small hand clutching his. Angela had the strangest feeling that the world had stopped on its axis, the strangest feeling that Dominic was struggling with himself, wrestling with himself, trying to make a decision. A decision that for him was unbelievably difficult to make.

But in the end his features relaxed in a smile, a smile that creased his cheeks and warmed his green eyes. He ruffled Nicky's hair casually, dishevelling the neatly brushed strands, and said, 'Sounds great, Nick. I've never seen a swinging bridge before.' Then, with Nicky's little hand enclosed in his big one, he uncoiled his tall figure from his chair and got to his feet. 'But let's give your Grandpa a hand first with the dishes,' he suggested, 'and then we can all go——'

Graeme waved away his protests. 'No, no,' he said firmly. 'Off you go. I'll cycle up the river myself when I'm finished, and meet you at the bridge.'

Angela looked down at the floor. To her surprise, the faded old lino was still there, just as it had been for as long as she could remember. Why was it, then, that she felt as if the world—her world—was giving way under her? Her father had accepted Dominic, and Nicky had accepted Dominic. And Dominic had accepted them both. She felt as if she was losing control of her life...and the people she loved.

Feeling tears prick her eyes, she got up quickly from her chair. 'Excuse me a minute.' Blindly she made for the door. 'I...I'll go up and get my sandals on.'

By the time she came back downstairs, she felt a little less distraught. Today was soon going to be over, she reassured herself, and things would once more go back to the way they had been before. There would be just her father, and Nicky, and herself. They neither needed nor wanted anyone else in their lives.

Straightening her shoulders, she crossed the hall. The front door was open, and she could see Nicky sitting on his bike on the path leading to the front gate. As she stepped outside, she noticed Dominic leaning against the old apple tree in the middle of the lawn, his hands in his trouser pockets. He was looking at Nicky, his expression absent, and thoughtful. But a moment later, when Nicky rang his bike bell and grinned at him, Dominic grinned back, his green eyes friendly.

Angela felt a seed of panic plant itself inside her as she saw the beginnings of an unmistakable rapport grow between the two. Get out of our lives, she wanted to cry to Dominic. Don't you dare make my son start to love you——

'Ready?' Dominic had noticed her; he now raised a mocking dark eyebrow in her direction.

'Yes,' she said coolly. 'I'm ready. Come on, Nicky.' Her voice was sharper than she intended. 'Let's go.' She unlatched the front gate. 'Stop when you come to the pillarbox and wait for us to catch up.'

'Righto, Mummy!' With the cheery words, he was away, pedalling furiously as the bike's little training wheels wobbled along on either side.

She would have to walk with Dominic, she acknowledged, but she didn't have to talk with him. Following Nicky with brisk steps, she tried to ignore the man striding along beside her. But no matter how fast she walked he stuck to her, just like the shadow he'd promised her he'd be.

'You've made a good job of bringing the boy up.' Dominic's tone was strained. 'He seems like a fine lad.'

'He is.' Despite herself, Angela's voice softened. 'He's a joy.'

For a minute or two, they walked in silence. Then Dominic went on, 'Your father was saying you continued your education after he was born. I seem to recall you'd planned to teach. Did you——?'

'No.' Angela stared straight ahead and kept walking at the same fast pace. 'I didn't go to university—it was out of the question. Oh, I could have—my father wanted me to—offered to take out a mortgage to pay for my fees——'

'You turned him down?'

'Of course.' Angela flung him a hard look. 'My father worked long and hard for many years to pay off the mortgage on the cottage—I wasn't about to let him take on another one. Why should *he* have had to pay for a mistake *I* made?'

'And the child's father...' Dominic's voice was suddenly harsh '...you never considered approaching him for money?'

'No.' She sensed he was waiting for her to say more, but she stubbornly maintained a silence. In the end, he was the one to speak.

'That surprises me.'

'I don't know why it should.' Angela tried to maintain a cool demeanour, but she realised she'd clenched her hands into fists, and so she stuck them into the slash pockets of her sweatshirt. 'In the circumstances,' she added coldly, 'he was the last person I could ask for help.'

'You made a big mistake, didn't you, Angela, allowing yourself to become pregnant? You might eventually have got everything you wanted, had you just bided your time.'

The anger Angela had been trying to contain suddenly broke to the surface. 'What I should like to know,' she returned accusingly, 'is why you're involving yourself with me now. From the way you acted in the past, I'd have thought you'd want to keep as much distance between us as possible. What game are you playing, Dominic?'

They had almost caught up with Nicky. Dominic's gaze fixed on the boy as he answered, quietly so that Nicky wouldn't hear him, 'It's no game. I'm only making sure you don't cause any trouble. Your shadow, Angela, my sweet—that's what I am, and what I promised you I was going to be this weekend. After the christening, I'll drive you to catch your train, I'll stay on the platform till it leaves, to make sure you're still on it . . . and then——' he shrugged '—we shan't ever have to see each other again. Oh——' he slanted a contemptuous glance at her '—just one other thing. Before you leave, I'll have your sworn oath that you'll keep away from the Hall. And this time I expect you to abide by your word.'

'Come on, Mummy.' Nicky's voice broke into the tension vibrating between them. 'Let's go up the river now.'

Angela moved abruptly away from Dominic and crossed to where Nicky stood, at the gate leading to the riverside path. Her heartbeats were hammering twenty to the dozen...yet she felt a great relief rippling through her. Her fears regarding Nicky had been needless. Dominic had no intention of trying to make Nicky love him, no intention of trying to weasel his way into her life again. But, in addition to the tremendous feeling of relief, to her dismay she had to acknowledge that she also felt a queer sinking feeling in the pit of her stomach. A sinking feeling that she had to admit might be disappointment. Surely there wasn't a part of her that was foolish enough, crazy enough, to want to see this man after today? Hadn't she learned her lesson?

'Allow me.' Dominic's arm brushed hers as he held the gate open for her, his breath warm against her cheeks as she squeezed past him.

'Thanks,' she muttered vaguely. What was happening to her? What was happening to her firm resolution not to make herself vulnerable to him again? She heard the gate swing shut, and at the same time sensed he was once more by her side. Leave me alone, she wanted to cry; go away.

But she couldn't, not with Nicky there.

Forcing a smile as Nicky called to her to hurry, she started along the edge of the river, barely hearing the pleasant ripple of the water as it bubbled swiftly over the rounded stones of the riverbed. All she could think of was this man beside her, and the shocking fact that, despite his arrogance and cruelty, he still had the power to ensnare her with his male magnetism and set her blood churning with just one feather-light touch.

'Come on, Dominic!' Nicky's childish voice called shrilly. 'Come on to the bridge.'

Angela blinked back to awareness of her surroundings; she'd been so lost in her thoughts that she hadn't noticed they had arrived at the swinging bridge. Nicky had parked his bike by an oak tree, and was standing in the centre of the bridge, looking down at the river in the gully below. The bridge, fashioned from rope and planks in a crude but sturdy way, was rocking gently, but, when she and Dominic stepped on to it, it began to sway more wildly.

Angela stumbled and would have lost her balance as she grabbed for the rope barrier, but Dominic moved swiftly and caught her around the waist when she was more than halfway down. She felt strong-muscled arms lifting her upright, as if she were a fragile doll, felt hard, relentless hands hold her when they could have—should have—let her go.

'Are you all right?' His face was close to hers, his eyes concerned. She could smell his hair, his skin—they smelled of apples and sunshine. As he spoke he moved his hands a little, and—accidentally, she was sure—they touched the swell of her breasts.

She felt her eyelids flutter as a tingle ran through her flesh. Her voice was raspy as she said, 'I'm fine.'

She didn't know how long they stood there, eyes locked, his fingertips just inches from her nipples. His breathing was ragged, his eyes darkening by the moment. She tasted his breath on her lips, felt his fingers tremble. And she felt her own body tremble. With yearning. A yearning such as she'd never known before, and it tore at her so desperately that she almost cried out in anguish. All she wanted to do at that moment was surrender to him, put her arms around him, feel his muscled back under her palms, feel his heartbeats against her cheek, feel him cup his hands around her breasts——

'Look, there's Grandpa!'

Nicky's shriek of excitement shattered the erotic tension vibrating between them. Sliding his hands away with the kind of natural gesture he'd have made had he just been righting a lifeless statue, Dominic stepped back.

Angela did too, and saw her father coming along the path on his bike. He wouldn't have noticed anything, she was sure...he was too far away to have seen the desire that had darkened Dominic's eyes, too far away to have seen the way her body had arched towards the man holding her.

'I'm going to meet Grandpa!' Grinning as he ran back along the bridge, Nicky passed them on his way. He ran to his bike and, climbing on, pedalled furiously back along the path to join his grandfather. A few moments later, they were passing the end of the bridge together.

Graeme waved, and shouted, 'I'll take the lad further up the river. See you in a while.'

Angela watched till they disappeared from view behind a stand of larch trees, waited till the sound of their tyres crunching on the path had faded, and then, compelled by a force over which she had no power, she turned, slowly, to look at Dominic.

He was gazing down into the water, his profile to her...a profile so beautiful that it made her heart ache. The lines so strong, so rugged...

He turned and their eyes locked. Angela felt a spasm of desire quiver through her, so intensely that it made the breath catch in her throat. She swallowed, and looked away.

'What are you thinking about?' he asked abruptly.

For a moment she didn't answer, just listened to the sound of the water tinkling and rushing below. Then after a while, when she could be sure her voice would sound normal, she said, 'What was I thinking about? Oh . . . just how strange life can be. How things can . . . change.'

'Things?'

'Oh . . . Patsy, for example,' she murmured, trying not to sound evasive. 'At one time, we were inseparable, and being with her yesterday made me realise how I've missed her——'

'You have only yourself to blame for that!'

She didn't answer at first, and then she said, staring blindly down into the swiftly moving stream below, 'Dominic, there's one thing I've always wanted to ask you——'

'Ask away,' he said roughly.

'That night by the lake, when we . . .' She hesitated, unable to say the words.

'When we made love?' His voice was taut.

'Yes,' she went on, quietly, 'when we . . . made love. Had you taken me there to see whether I would . . . succumb to your advances . . . or fight them?' She raised her head and looked up at him, and all her bitterness seemed to disappear, leaving only a deep sadness inside her. 'Was it a . . . test?'

'A *test*? What the hell are you talking about?' Dominic rubbed a hand over his nape in a distracted gesture. 'Of course it wasn't a bloody test! What kind of a man do you think I am?'

'I just wondered . . . if perhaps it was something you did when you began to get serious about a girl—take her to the lake, see if she was "easy" or not, and then if she was you'd just...' Her words trailed away.

She saw a look of pain in his eyes; it was only there for a moment, and then it was gone. 'You want an answer to your question? No,' he said, 'no, I didn't think...that night...that you were easy.'

Shaking her head, Angela moved past him, and began walking back along the narrow bridge, causing it to sway again. 'No,' she said, almost to herself, 'I didn't see how you could. After all, it was the first time for me...'

The unhappiness in her tone must have reached out to him, because she found herself grasped by the arms and pulled her round to face him. 'There was nothing wrong with that night,' he said savagely. 'It was what happened af——' He broke off, shaking his head. 'Forget it!'

He wasn't making sense...but then, when had she ever understood him? Angela felt tears rush to her eyes, felt her lips tremble. And as she did she heard him swear.

'For God's sake, Angela, don't look like that...'

The hands that had been grasping her arms slid roughly around her back, drawing her close. Again she smelled the fragrance of apples and sunshine, but now, as his unshaven jaw rasped against her soft skin, underlying the fragrance of shampoo and soap was the potent scent of male musk that was distinctively his own. As it infiltrated Angela's nostrils, it brought a pleading, animal sound from her throat, a sound that seemed to demolish Dominic's self-control.

With a helpless groan, he slipped his hands up over her shoulders and threaded them through her hair, pressing feverish kisses to her cheeks, her temples, her eyelids. She could feel the warmth of the sun on her back, feel the breeze lifting her hair...feel the blood rush hot and wild in her veins as Dominic dragged his mouth back to hers.

His lips were full and moist and persuasive, and as they moved compellingly, possessively on hers she found her own lips parting in breathless invitation, opening to him recklessly, welcoming the intimate intrusion of his tongue, the aggressive snake-like twining of his flesh around hers, teasing, provoking, arousing...

She was only barely aware that she was on her tiptoes, arching against him, her burning need to feel the shape of his body against hers like a fire that had to be fed. Her fingers were in his hair, desperately tangled in the thick, rich strands, her body was moulded against his. She knew there were sounds around them—the ripple of the water below, the breeze rustling the leaves of the larches, the creak of the bridge as it swayed gently with their movements—but she heard nothing. Nothing but the heavy thudding of her heart, nothing but the barely audible sound of their lips as their kiss became a stormy, reckless mating——

She cried out in protest when he wrenched himself away. 'No!' The throaty sound was like a call for help. Why was he no longer holding her, why was no longer kissing her, why had he taken her wrists and pulled her arms down——?

'They're coming back.' His voice was low but forceful. 'Listen.'

Angela stared up into his eyes, catching her ragged breath as she listened. She let it out in a shuddering sigh. 'Yes,' she whispered, 'I hear them.' She, too—later than he—had heard the faint crunch of the bicycle wheels on the path.

And just as she stepped back, and raked a trembling hand through her hair to tidy it, the two figures appeared around the bend, and a tinkling noise broke into the tense silence: Nicky, ringing the bell on his little bike. He waved when he saw them, and the bike wobbled precariously.

Somehow, Angela found the strength to wave back, but, though she was smiling, her voice held no laughter as she spoke to Dominic.

'The minute we get back to the cottage,' she said, her voice still slightly unsteady, 'you and I will leave for the Hall. And as far as I'm concerned the sooner we get there the better. I don't know what you're trying to prove, Dominic, but whatever it is I don't want to be any part of it. If it's sex you want, you'll have to look elsewhere—I'm not interested, and it's a mystery to me why you would want to make love to me, considering the way I feel about you. I don't even *like* you, Dominic.'

Swinging her arms angrily by her sides—and, not quite sure whether her anger was directed at Dominic or herself, or both of them—she walked along the path towards Nicky. She was aware that Dominic was following her closely, but she ignored him. Ruffling Nicky's fair hair when she reached him, she said lightly, 'Had a good ride, darling? We have to go back to the cottage now. I'm afraid Dominic is in a hurry to leave—he has an appointment at home that he forgot about—so we'll have to be on our way.'

Her father, she suddenly noticed, was looking at Dominic with a smug look in his eyes . . . looking at his mouth, it seemed. Automatically, she followed his gaze . . . and realised Dominic must have been aware of the smug look too. He rubbed a hand against his lips, and she saw the faint hint of pink on his skin. Lipstick. *Her* lipstick. She cursed under her breath.

'Aye, lad,' Graeme said, with a twinkle in his eye, 'you'd best be going. But I won't say goodbye, because I've a feeling you'll be back. And soon.'

Humming happily, he set off on his old bike again, his cardigan flapping behind him as he rode.

No, Angela thought dully, you're wrong. He won't be coming back here.

But even as she made that promise to herself she wondered what she would do if Dominic ever *did* decide to return to Hawthorne Cottage.

Would she be able to stop him?

CHAPTER FIVE

STARR and Max were coming down the drive in Starr's antique Rolls, Max driving, when Dominic swung his BMW off the main road and in between the huge stone lions guarding the entrance to Hadleigh Hall. Max slowed down, and, with her hair dancing in the breeze, Starr called to them as the two vehicles passed each other, 'We're going to the village for the Sunday papers.'

Dominic called back, 'See you shortly, then,' and with an effort Angela threw them a bright smile.

The journey from Hawthorne Cottage had been a strain. Dominic had suggested stopping for coffee when they'd driven through one of the small towns *en route*, but she had turned down the invitation with a cool, 'I think you've forgotten what I said earlier. The less time I have to spend in your company, the better pleased I shall be.' She'd seen him compress his lips into a thin line, and as soon as they'd left the confines of the town and hit the open road again he'd gunned the car till they were riding just on the speed-limit, and he hadn't spoken another word till he'd returned Starr's greeting a moment ago.

Well, they were here at last, and she would be able to get away from him and go to her room. Perhaps there she could manage to relax, and get rid of the awful churning in her stomach.

But as she got out of the car and walked quickly away from him she heard the crunch of his steps behind her and a second later felt his hand on her arm.

'Just a minute,' he snapped, roughly pulling her to a halt. 'Not so fast——'

She jerked herself free and glared up at him. 'Will you stop *doing* that? Stop grabbing me, as if I were a——'

'I wouldn't have to,' he said in silky tones, 'if you would do as you're told. You're forgetting what I told you earlier—I'm your shadow, Angela, my pet, so don't make it hard for me. Don't try to slip away——'

'Darlings!' Patsy had appeared at the top of the front-door steps. 'You're back. And just in time to have a glass of wine before we go through for lunch.'

Taking the opportunity to escape, Angela moved quickly up the steps. 'That sounds lovely,' she said, forcing a smile. 'I'll just run upstairs and wash my hands first.'

'Don't take too long,' Patsy said with a chuckle, 'I've *missed* you. And I'm going to need you for moral support—Mummy phoned earlier—she's got some ghastly stomach bug and can't come to the christening. I would put it off, but of course I can't—it's too late— so many people are coming and some, like Max, from so far away.'

'Oh, Patsy, what a pity.'

'Mmm...but can't be helped, unfortunately. And thank goodness it's nothing serious...sounds like a twenty-four-hour flu. But your dad—we were so worried last night, till Dominic called and put our minds at rest. He's all right?'

'Oh, yes, he's back to his usual chirpy self this morning.' Angela looped her arm through her friend's as they walked into the house. Dominic was right behind, and Angela felt as aware of him as if he were a huge dark cloud just waiting to burst and deluge her with freezing rain. 'The four of us had a lovely walk after breakfast, before Dominic and I left.'

But even as Patsy said, 'The four of you?', and even as Angela bit her lip at her slip Dominic interjected in a casual voice,

'Graeme has a friend next door—Molly.'

Oh, very clever. Angela had to hand it to him; he hadn't lied, but had certainly implied that Molly had been the fourth member of their little outing.

Patsy chuckled. 'Ah... and are they... romantically involved?'

'Oh, heavens, no!' Angela smiled. 'They're just good friends. They've known each other since Molly rented the little bungalow next door three years ago, and they spend a lot of time together at the park because——' Oh, lord, she had been going to say because her father liked taking Nicky there and Molly seemed to enjoy being with them.

But before she could Dominic had interjected again.

'They both have a liking for the outdoors,' he said.

Angela decided she had best get on upstairs before she said something she shouldn't. She could feel Dominic's hand on the small of her back... it would look, she knew, like a casual gesture, but she could feel the hard warning of his fingertips as they dug into her flesh.

'I'll be down in a couple of minutes, Patsy,' she said, and, wriggling irritably from Dominic's touch, she made for the stairs.

'I'll be waiting here for you.' Dominic's voice reached her as she got to the landing. Looking down, she saw that Patsy had gone and Dominic was standing there on his own, watching her. His head was tilted arrogantly, his hands thrust just as arrogantly into his pockets.

With a defiant toss of her head, Angela turned away. She would make sure that when she came down again she'd keep as far from him as possible. And it shouldn't be too difficult to avoid him for the rest of her time at the Hall. The christening was to be in the early afternoon, and she would be able to leave shortly afterwards. If Dominic insisted on being the one to drive her to the train, there wasn't much she could do about that. And, after all, she'd been thankful enough for his services last night, when she'd so desperately needed a drive to the hospital.

But once she got on the train she'd try to forget all about him. It should be a lot easier now, now that she knew he wasn't the slightest bit interested in Nicky, or in taking Nicky from her.

It *should* be easier, she thought...

But she had an ominous feeling that it was going to be even more difficult than it had been in the past.

It might even be impossible.

'It's too bad,' Mike frowned as he sipped from his wine glass, 'that Patsy's mum can't be here this afternoon. She's been longing for today.'

'It's too bad you hadn't known earlier that she couldn't come,' Angela offered, 'or you could have rented a video camera and taped the christening for her.'

'There's a shop in the village that rents out equipment——' Patsy began, but Dominic broke in flatly, 'It's not open on a Sunday. Nothing is around here, except the newsagent's.'

Mike laid his wine glass on the table by his side. 'Patsy, Starr used to have a video camera, didn't she? Remember that time when we were fooling around with it——'

'I remember!' Angela chuckled. '*Love's Dark Shadow*!'

'Oh, what a hoot that was!' Patsy looked up at Dominic, the only one not seated around the hearth. He was standing leaning against the wall by the fire, one elbow on the mantelpiece. 'You weren't here, Dominic. It was just before Mike and I got married. Angela was here, and Starr had just bought a video camera, and——'

'You can tell Dominic later,' Mike interrupted good-naturedly. 'The thing we have to find out right now is...does Starr still have it?'

'Does Starr still have what?' Starr's familiar voice came from the open doorway, where she had appeared with Max, who had a sheaf of Sunday papers under one arm.

'Your video camera!' Mike got to his feet. 'We thought we could tape the christening, for Patsy's mum.'

'What a marvellous idea! Oh, I'm sure I still have it somewhere, but I haven't used it in ages. Lord knows where it is. Nelly might, though.' She smiled as she mentioned the housekeeper. 'You can ask the old dear to go look for it, if you like.' She made a dismissing gesture and, drawing Max into the room with her, she crossed to one of the low couches, and said, 'But first, darling, do pour us a drink.'

Max settled beside her, and immersed himself right away in one of the newspapers. Absent-mindedly, he extricated the leisure pages for Starr, and, toying with one of her pearl earrings, she began scrutinising photographs taken at a recent fashion show.

Patsy looked at her watch. 'I'm going to see if Nanny has brought the baby back from his walk,' she said to Mike, as he brought two glasses of wine and laid them on the coffee-table in front of Starr and Max. 'Will you go and search out Nelly, and ask her to look for the video camera?'

'Sure. Excuse us a sec, will you?' Mike put an arm around Patsy's shoulders, and together they left the room.

Angela could sense Dominic's penetrating eyes fixed on her, and, irritated because it made her feel self-conscious, she put her glass on the hearth and got up. With a murmured 'Excuse me' to Starr and Max, she walked across the large room to the open french doors, ignoring Dominic as she did so, and moved out on to the patio. The day was pleasant, although there was a distinct autumn nip to the air. She shivered a little in the cool breeze . . . but getting chilled out here, she decided, was preferable to sitting indoors with Dominic's hostile green stare boring right into her.

Wandering along one of the little paths criss-crossing the rose garden, she had just paused for a moment to inspect a pink rambler she and Mr Elliott had planted years before when she heard Dominic's mocking voice right behind her.

'Pink roses . . . the flowers of romance.'

Angela took in a deep breath. He'd really meant it, hadn't he, when he'd warned her he was going to be her shadow while she was at the Hall? Her thoughts, of their own accord, flitted to the past, when she would have given her soul to have had Dominic Elliott promise he'd be by her side constantly. How times had changed, she mused bitterly.

'Do you have romance in your life, Angela?'

Why couldn't he leave her alone? Wearily, she turned and looked at him, and felt the breath catch in her throat. With the sunshine picking up the glossy highlights of his black hair and lighting up his strong, arrogant features, he looked so harshly attractive that she felt stunned.

And not only stunned, but threatened by the powerful sensual waves that emanated from him. Clasping her arms around herself protectively, she said, in a voice that came out threadily, 'I don't think that's any business of yours.'

'No,' he said, 'I suppose it isn't. Still. . .' His eyes raked over her, but she could see no emotion there, just a cool, assessing hardness. 'You are very beautiful, so I must assume you're not lacking in admirers. You suit red,' he said unexpectedly, 'but then you always did.' Before she could move back, he'd reached out and touched the soft fabric of her sweatshirt, his fingertips coming perilously close to her breasts. 'You had a dress, once, the same colour as this, didn't you? Or perhaps I'm thinking of some other girl . . .' he flicked the fabric carelessly before dropping his hand '. . . some other dress?'

She knew the dress he was referring to, and she felt pain twist inside her; it was the dress she'd worn that night by the lake. He had loved it, had said he'd never seen one as beautiful. . . now he was pretending he didn't even remember if it was her or someone else who had worn it. Why was he so determined to hurt her? Did he take pleasure from her pain? Well, if so she was damned if she'd let him have that satisfaction.

'No,' she said steadily, 'not another girl, not another dress. I did have one this colour——'

'Red...the colour of desire.' He laughed, a contemptuous sound. 'Everyone knows that red is supposed to provoke passion in men. It worked for you, didn't it? Do you still have it, that lucky dress?'

'No,' she said, 'I don't.' How he'd crow if he knew she'd eventually sent it to a jumble sale, unable to face the memories that had torn at her every time she wore it.

'Pity——'

'Darlings...' Starr's voice came floating towards them from the patio. 'Lunch is served. Do come, or Cook's going to have a fit!'

Angela realised that Dominic was looking down at her with a sardonic smile. 'That we must avoid at all costs! Here——' he crooked an arm and held it out to her '—take my arm.'

Angela ignored the proffered arm, and, giving him a cool glance, said, 'Excuse me,' and walked past him.

He hadn't shaved that morning at Hawthorne Cottage though her father had offered him a razor; he'd waited till his return to the Hall, and as she passed him she was subjected to both his own male scent and the tantalising fragrance of his aftershave. The sensual combination had her senses reeling. She could almost feel on her skin a million tiny invisible antennae flailing wildly in the air, seeking out the source of this erotically intoxicating potion. There was something about this man, she acknowledged to herself despairingly, that, despite his despicable behaviour, still drew her to him with a magnetism that was well nigh irresistible.

She had to clench her hands into fists and jam them into her pockets to prevent them from betraying her as she was assaulted by a sudden irrational desire to slide her arms around his waist. But even with her hands safely tucked in her pockets she was then almost overwhelmed by an intense craving to pull his shirt-tails out of his trousers, slide her fingers up over his bare back, feel his naked flesh beneath her palms.

Pheromones...

A self-derisive smile tugged down the corners of her lips. Foolish woman, she chastised herself grimly, as she walked by him and entered the house, even to think of allowing herself to be seduced by nature's secret weapon.

Dominic Elliott had already shown her all too clearly what he thought of women who succumbed to his sexual charm.

Surely she was old enough that she didn't have to be taught the same lesson twice?

After lunch, when Dominic made to detain her as they were all leaving the dining-room, Angela was relieved when Patsy said, 'I know it's foolish but I'm getting rather nervous about the ceremony. Do you mind, Dominic, darling, if I steal Angela away while I get the baby ready for the christening? I need her moral support, now that Mum's not going to be here with me.'

'Excuse me, Dominic.' Angela was not in the least ashamed of the smug little smile she threw him as she sailed from the room, arm in arm with Patsy.

'What's *going on* with you two?' Patsy whispered as they crossed the hall together.

'Don't ask,' Angela said with a weary shake of her head. 'For some reason known only to his lordship, he's determined not to let me out of his sight till I leave.'

'Does he think you're planning to steal the family jewels?'

'You tell me.' Angela shrugged helplessly. 'Anyhow, let's not waste our time talking about it. Whatever his problem is, it'll obviously be over after I leave.'

'It's so unlike him,' Patsy murmured as they reached the landing. 'Dominic's usually so cool, so controlled. In fact, I'd have to say that's always been his most dominant characteristic. Throw him into any emotional situation, and he'll not only stop and count to ten, he'll

stop and count to a hundred...and even then he'll step
back and avoid confrontation—it's just not his style.
Given the existing circumstances between you two, I'd
have bet a thousand to one that he'd have been coolly
polite to you this weekend, because it's not in his nature
to be rude, and that he'd have gone to all ends to avoid
being in your company. Yet...he's doing the opposite——'

'You're right,' Angela agreed, 'he's following me like
a shadow, and as for being polite——'

'Would obnoxious be a better word?'

They both laughed, and were still chuckling as Patsy
opened the door to the nursery.

'Is he awake, Nanny?' Patsy addressed the plump, red-
haired woman folding nappies at a table by the window.

'Awake, ma'am, and changed, and ready for his feed.'

'Thanks, Nanny. Off you go now, and have a cup of
tea. I won't need you till..oh, around three. Everyone
will want to goo and gaa over the baby once the
christening's over, but after that I'll bring him up here.'

Angela moved over to the crib with Patsy as the door
shut behind the nanny. 'May I hold him?' she asked.

'Sure.' Patsy lifted him out of the lace-trimmed crib
and, after brushing a kiss on the baby's brow, handed
him to her friend. 'Which arm?'

'This one,' Angela replied automatically, cradling the
infant in her left arm, smiling as a pair of cloudy eyes
tried to focus on her.

'"To the manner born",' Patsy commented. 'You look
as if you'd been holding babies all your life.'

Angela cursed herself for not having fumbled at least
a little when she took the child. 'I love babies,' she said,
affecting a casual smile. 'I think holding babies comes
naturally to anyone who is fond of them.'

'You're right,' Patsy agreed, as she gazed adoringly
at her infant. 'Some men are such klutzes with kids...I
half expected Mike would be one of those, and I was
delighted to find he wasn't. But it's Dominic who really

surprised me! He's become so brooding and withdrawn these past few years, I thought he'd just glower down at his nephew and mutter a few polite words. I could have just melted the first time I saw him with the baby—and did you notice yesterday how he beamed when little Dominic gurgled up at him, and how delighted he was when the baby grabbed his finger and wouldn't let go? ''There's a man,'' I said to myself, ''who should have children. He would make a wonderful father!'' Don't you agree?'

'Mmm.' Angela tried to cope with all the emotions that had welled up inside her as she listened to Patsy's cheerful chatter. Dominic *is* a father, she could have said. *The father of my child.* She could have said it . . . but she wouldn't. Dominic had warned her not to, and, after all, he was the one who would be most affected if the news came out. So instead of confiding in her old friend, as she would have dearly loved to do, she just gave the baby a last cuddle and handed him back.

'Let's sit on the window-seat,' Patsy said, and, sitting down, she undid her blouse and, unfastening her nursing bra, began feeding the baby. 'And now... you were telling me yesterday morning that you've just started a new job. Tell me more. How did you find it?'

'When I finished the horticultural course at Brantwell College, I spent ages looking for work but just couldn't find anything in my line. Finally, a few months ago, I heard about an opening at a garden centre in Brockton, and I was lucky enough to be hired. It's not the best job in the world, but I was glad to get it.'

'You always did like grubbing around in the earth. I remember when you helped Dom plant the rose garden.'

Angela smiled as she remembered. 'Yes, that was fun. More fun than the work I'm doing at present—I have to spend a lot of time in the shop, selling fertilisers and seeds and weed-killer——'

'Yuk!'

'Yuk, indeed! But it pays quite well. And I get along well with my supervisor, so there's not much likelihood of my being fired. I value the security.'

Little Dominic pulled his lips from Patsy's engorged nipple and milk gurgled from his lips. With a smile, Patsy draped a nappy over her shoulder and, propping him against it, rubbed his back gently. She didn't say anything for a minute, but when she did her eyes were bright.

'Would you consider working in the gardens here, at Hadleigh Hall?'

'Oh, no! I couldn't——'

'I'm sorry, Angela.' Patsy bit her lip. 'Golly, I feel awful . . . this is so awkward. We've been friends for so long . . . and I'm asking you to work for me . . .'

'Oh, that's not why I said no!' Angela shook her head. 'It's just . . . I thought you meant . . . I should ask Dominic if he would give me a job. After all, the Hall does belong to him, doesn't it?'

There was a long silence, and, to Angela's horror, she saw Patsy's eyes fill with tears. Taking a tissue from a packet on the dresser beside her, the other woman dabbed at her eyes. 'Oh, Angela . . .' Her voice broke, and she stopped, obviously unable to go on.

'What on earth's the matter?' Angela had never seen her friend cry before. It was a shock . . . what could she possibly have to cry about? She was very happily married to a man she loved, she had a darling baby . . .

'You'll find out this afternoon—I wasn't going to talk about it, but . . . oh, Angela, Mike and I have had so many fights about it——'

'About what?' As she asked the question, Angela recalled all of a sudden the tension she'd sensed several times in the atmosphere, the undercurrents, the anguished look she'd seen on Mike's face, the distress on Angela's. 'Look, you don't have to talk about it if it's going to upset you——'

'It's the Hall.' Patsy, her face now pale and composed, put the baby to her other breast, and in a moment he was sucking voraciously. 'Mike and Dominic always believed that, because Dominic was the elder son, when their father died Dominic would inherit Hadleigh Hall——'

'I did too!' Angela broke in. 'When I played chess with old Mr Elliott, he said more than once that Dominic would inherit the place when he died.'

'He changed his mind... and he changed his will.' Patsy's huge eyes were filled with sadness. 'He wrote a new one, just weeks before he died. The doctors had told him he hadn't long to live, but he told no one except Starr. Anyway, it was common knowledge that his dearest wish was that there always be a Dominic Elliott at Hadleigh Hall, and, with the terms of his new will, he did his best to achieve that. He divided his financial assets equally among Starr, Dominic and Mike... but the actual estate—Hadleigh Hall and the thousand acres surrounding it—was to go to the first of his sons to father a male child, the condition being that the boy be christened Dominic. I think he was afraid Dominic would never marry, and he was trying to force his hand.'

Angela found herself staring disbelievingly into Patsy's swimming eyes, but even as she took in the startling news she felt her brain, and her heart, reeling from the devastating implications.

It was only dimly that she heard Patsy go on in a tearful voice, 'Oh, Angela, we don't want the Hall. Mike has never wanted that responsibility. I've never told anyone this... and don't breathe it to a soul, or Mike will kill me—but he's been writing for years and years—mysteries—and has finally had a novel accepted, by one of the big publishers in New York——'

'Oh, how wonderful for him!'

'It is wonderful. All he's ever wanted to do is write. But Dominic——' Angela's voice trembled '—the Hadleigh Estate has always been his life. He loves it. He loves managing it, loves the horses, the stables——'

'Then why don't they, Dominic and Mike, come to some other arrangement? I mean, just because it was in the will, doesn't mean it's carved in stone. Can't Mike just sell it to Dominic—or does Dominic not have enough money?'

'Oh, Dominic's *loaded*!'

'Well, would that not be a simple solution?'

'It would be a simple solution,' Patsy said with a hopeless sigh, 'if those two weren't such...honourable men. They consider their father's will in the same way as a deathbed wish and neither one of them will do otherwise than he requested. They loved him...as we all did. Oh, Mike and I have argued about it, over and over. I told him that if he hadn't kept his writing a secret his father would never have expected him to sacrifice his chosen career, but——'

'Yes, knowing Mike...and Dominic...I can see how they must feel...'

'If only Dominic had had a child.' Patsy looked wistfully down at her baby, who stared back at her with unblinking eyes. 'There would have been no problem. Of course, now it's too late—our baby came first. I wanted to name him Michael—that would have been a way out of our dilemma——'

'Why, yes, of course it would! What a brilliant idea, Patsy. Wouldn't Mike go along with it?'

'Oh, he was thrilled at first...till he told Dominic, and Dominic said he never intended marrying, never intended bringing a child into the world. So of course, if we called our son Michael, we would really have been cheating. Our son will eventually be the heir to Hadleigh Hall, and Dom wanted that child to be named after him.'

Patsy sank back on the window-seat, her head resting on the pane. She herself, she realised with a sense of panic, and only she, had a way out of their dilemma. She had a son who was baptised Dominic...but Dominic had forbidden her to tell anyone of his existence. How strange...and how confusing. She felt her thoughts

jumble around in her brain and they just wouldn't make
sense. If, as Patsy had said, Dominic's life was the Hall,
why hadn't he brought his son here, and taken possession of his inheritance? It was beyond her
comprehension.

But she could understand Patsy's sorrow. She could
feel for her. Opening her eyes, she watched as Patsy eased
the now sleeping baby to her shoulder and burped him
again.

'Oh, Patsy,' she murmured, 'I'm so sorry.'

'I know, and it's a help just to be able to talk about
it with you.' Patsy managed a wan smile. 'I've kept it
cooped up inside for so long. Starr wanted it kept a secret
till today, till after the christening. She wanted to make
sure everything went smoothly, before telling everyone
about it.'

'Have Dominic and Mike been running the estate
together since their father died?'

'Mmm. Those were the terms of the will. But somehow
Dominic took charge—you know how he is. And of
course that suited Mike admirably. He didn't have the
responsibility thrust on his shoulders, so he had a clear
mind to enable him to get on with his writing in his leisure
time. But now...' Patsy heaved a heavy sigh, and
shrugged her shoulders despairingly.

'He's going to be miserable.'

'And when he's miserable I'm miserable. Most miserable of all, though, will be Dominic. Naturally, he
could continue working here, could actually, with Mike's
blessing, run the damned estate. But, knowing Dominic,
he wouldn't do that. He's too much his own man. Lord
knows what he'll do. He'll leave... but where will he go?
He'll be like a lost soul.'

'I wonder...'

'Wonder what?' Patsy encouraged, as Angela didn't
go on.

Angela grimaced. 'Well, if the Hall is so important to
Dominic, why in heaven's name didn't he make some

attempt to secure it? I mean, it's almost five years since his father died and the terms of his will were revealed—so why hasn't Dominic married and produced an heir?'

'I've often wondered about that,' Patsy murmured. 'It's certainly not for a lack of available women who would be delighted to snag him as a husband. Actually, instead of looking for a wife, I'd say he's been doing the opposite. He's shown no interest whatsoever in the opposite sex since... well, since he broke off with you, now that I come to think of it. Yes... it was after that, that he seemed to change. Withdrew into himself, became brooding, morose...

'Ah, well, no point in talking about that now. It's not going to help.' Glancing at her watch, Patsy went on in a flat voice, 'And it's time you and I were getting dressed for the christening.' She laid the baby on the changing-table and turned to Angela. 'I'm so glad you're here,' she said. 'Thanks for listening. You're the best friend in the world.'

Some friend, Angela thought, as guilt cut into her heart. With just a few words, she could solve all Patsy's problems.

She couldn't do it, of course, because of Dominic.

But still...

Her heart aching, she looked at Patsy, whose attention was now focused on changing the baby into his christening robe. Patsy had always been faithful, dependable, supportive. Since the night at the lake, Dominic had been harsh, demanding, unforgiving. Which of the two deserved her loyalty?

It was in her power to make Patsy happy... and Mike too. But at what cost to herself? What penalty might Dominic exact if she crossed him? He had made no claim on Nicky... but might he not swing the other way, just to make her suffer? The new Dominic, the Dominic he had become, might indeed be vindictive enough to do that.

If Dominic tried to gain custody of Nicky, it was possible a judge might decide her child would be much better off with his father. Angela felt her heart twist with anguish at the prospect of life without Nicky.

Distraught, she walked to the window and looked out through eyes blurred with tears.

What was the right thing to do?

Oh, if only she knew.

CHAPTER SIX

THE christening ceremony went without a hitch. The baby gave one small cry of protest as he felt the drops of water fall on his brow, but lay sleepily in the minister's arms while the baptismal words were spoken over him.

Max had brought Starr's video camera and had placed himself unobtrusively at one side, making a record of the occasion. Angela, standing with Mike and Patsy, was all too aware of Dominic's presence, even as she listened to the words of dedication being pronounced. From the corner of her eye she could see his tall figure outlined against the sunlight slanting in through one of the mullioned windows. He was wearing a navy suit, with a light blue shirt and a navy and dark red striped tie, and he looked absolutely devastating. When he'd come into the drawing-room earlier and made straight for where she was standing, she'd had to grasp the back of the chair beside her to steady herself.

He had skimmed a glance over her as he crossed the room, and as he did she'd had the distinct feeling that he was mentally stripping her of her pink knit sweater and matching skirt, her sheer tights and her high-heeled pumps.

'You look good enough to eat,' he murmured, as he joined her.

Angela tried to ignore the peculiar tingling dancing across her skin, but realised she had clasped her arms around herself defensively. He slanted a smile down at her, a lazy, knowing smile that accelerated her heartbeats and brought a flush to her cheeks.

It was pure physical attraction, she reassured herself steadily, and something she had better ignore. Wasn't it that same sensual smile that had charmed her into believing she was in love with him, and he with her, when she'd succumbed to his passionate lovemaking by the lake that moonlit night? But a mature woman, such as she was now, knew that falling in love with a smile was a very foolish, and very dangerous, thing to do. Biting her lip, she turned away from him, and saw Patsy gesturing to her to come and stand beside her. With a clipped, 'Excuse me,' to Dominic, she moved away and took her place with Patsy. A few moments later, the ceremony had begun.

And now, thank heavens, it was over. Soon, she'd be able to leave...

'Ladies and gentlemen.' Gaily Starr drew everyone's attention to herself. 'Let's drink a toast to the baby. Mike, darling, open the champagne!'

Angela noticed that Starr, usually pale and poised, looked flushed and excited. Her hands were fluttering nervously, and her turquoise eyes had an almost feverish sparkle. Angela was aware that this was a very special day for the ex-actress—her son was to become owner of the Hall and this would ensure that she always had a home here. On the other hand, had the Hall come into Dominic's possession she would inevitably have had to assume a position of minor importance as she didn't have the same influence over him as she did over Mike. The terms of the will were, indeed, very much to her benefit.

Thinking back to the previous day, Angela suddenly recalled the tension in the air as Patsy had told Dominic about the change in the sleeping arrangements. It had been *Starr* who had moved Dominic from the master suite, Starr who had made the decision to put him in the Tower Suite. Was Starr trying to push Dominic out? Though Patsy had never acknowledged it in so many words, during the period of her engagement she had on several occasions shown signs that she was frustrated by the way Starr had tended to control and manipulate the easygoing, unassertive Mike. Angela hadn't given it much thought at the time, but now she couldn't help wondering if Starr wasn't perhaps one of those mothers-in-law who couldn't help interfering in their children's lives. And perhaps Patsy's distress about having to remain on at the Hall stemmed partly from the knowledge that Mike would still be under his mother's powerful influence.

Frowning, Angela halted her train of thought. It was none of her business . . . and just because she herself had never felt totally at ease around Starr was no reason for her to think nasty thoughts about her!

With an effort, she smiled in Mike's direction as she saw him approach her with a tray of champagne. But her smile faded as Dominic swooped two fluted glasses away and, murmuring something to Mike, wove his way over to her.

'Your drink, my lady,' he said.

'Thanks,' she said curtly, and turned her shoulder away from him a little. To her relief, she saw there was a couple standing next to her, and quickly she opened up a conversation with them.

'We're Maud and Harry Cranston,' the small balding man offered after she'd introduced herself. 'Haven't met you before. Not a local, are you?'

'No,' Angela said, turning even more, so that her back was to Dominic. 'I'm from Brockton.'

'Oh, Brockton. Nice little place. We passed through there, Maud, do ya remember, on our way north?'

'Yes, I remember. The roads were nice and quiet today for a change, weren't they, dear?' The woman, plump and friendly, smiled at Angela, and went on, 'I hope they're the same going back, don't you?'

'Oh, I'm not driving. I'm going back by train.'

'This afternoon?' Harry raised his gingery brows enquiringly.

'Mmm.'

'Why don't you come with us, dear? We're planning to leave around five. We have plenty of room, don't we, Harry? And we do love company!'

Opening her mouth to thank them for the invitation but decline it, as she really didn't feel like making polite conversation all the way to Brockton, she heard Dominic make a passing remark to someone behind her, and the sound of his voice reminded her that he was determined to drive her to the station.

'Why, that's very kind of you—that would be lovely! Thanks so much.'

'Good, that's settled.'

Angela felt Dominic's fingers curl round her forearm, and she turned to look up at him, an expression of innocence on her face.

His green eyes sparked with anger. 'There's no need for that,' he hissed. 'I told you I'd drive you to——'

'But these kind people are going to be driving past my door!' Angela returned with a lazy shrug of her shoulders.

'If I'd known you wanted to be driven home, I'd have offered to do so,' he said, his thin lips compressed. 'Tell them——'

'Everyone!' Starr's voice, high and slightly shrill, broke into the babble of conversation in the room. 'I think we all have our champagne now, so...let's raise our glasses and drink a toast—to baby Dominic, darling son of Mike and Patsy.'

'To baby Dominic!' There was a cheery clinking of glasses, and a sipping of champagne, but before conversation could break out again Starr went on, her cheeks as red as poppies now, 'This is a very happy day for our family, but it is also a day when I think with fondness of my late husband, Dom, and how he would have loved to be here with us on this occasion. It was his dearest wish that there always be a Dominic Elliott at Hadleigh Hall.' Starr paused, and, with a dainty, lace-trimmed handkerchief, dabbed her eyes. 'A wish that Mike and Patsy have granted. And because of this, and the terms of Dom's will—which state that the ownership of Hadleigh Hall and the Hadleigh Estate is to pass to whichever of his two sons has a son first, a son who is baptised Dominic—today Hadleigh Hall becomes . . .'

When Starr had started talking, Angela had felt her heart start to bump. Her stomach had heaved, and adrenalin had surged through her body, making her mouth turn dry. And, strangely, her senses had become intensely acute—it was as if she could see right into Mike, and Patsy, and Dominic, as her gaze darted in a panic from one to the other. Mike's face was as white as the linen cloth on the christening table, his eyes dark pools of unhappiness; Patsy's eyes shone with tears of despair; and Dominic's features were closed, clenched tight as a fist, as if he were making an agonising effort to keep whatever emotions he was feeling from showing on his face.

Speak now or forever hold your peace.

The words rocketed around and around in Angela's head like firecrackers. Her eyes shimmered, white lights streaked and zigzagged in front of her, and she knew with a dull feeling of acceptance that she was about to have one of her pole-axing migraines.

'Today,' Starr was repeating, going over the words again for dramatic effect, 'today Hadleigh Hall becomes the property of my son, M——'

'No!' Angela's voice was loud, though shaky. It drowned out Starr's voice and echoed through a room that had suddenly become deathly quiet. 'No,' she repeated, gripping the stem of her glass so tightly she was afraid it might snap. 'Not Mike. Dominic.'

Oh, God, she'd said it. Angela swallowed, and ran the tip of her tongue over her parched lips. Everyone had turned, everyone was looking at her, expressions of surprise on some faces, bewilderment on others, incredulity on yet others.

Starr was staring at her with a look of horror. Horror and outrage. Patsy and Mike were looking at her in dismay and bewilderment. Dominic . . .

But Angela didn't dare look at Dominic. Clearing her throat, she went on—and in the stunned silence the only sound in the room that she could hear was the terrifyingly rapid hammering of her own heart, 'Hadleigh Hall goes to Dominic because he also has a son...our son...who was born four years ago. I had him baptised in church when he was six weeks old. His name, too, is Dominic. Dominic Elliott. I called him after his grandfather.'

Now she *had* to turn to Dominic. She'd rather have sunk into a hole in the ground, but there was no hole deep enough to hide from him. Apprehension—no, more than apprehension...fear—came close to paralysing her as she gathered up all her remaining courage to do the thing that had to be done. How was he going to react to this bombshell she'd thrown? He could either laugh in her face and repudiate her claim, humiliate her before all these people, and tell her she was crazy—or he could admit the child was his child, and, by so doing, release Mike from a future filled with frustration, and Patsy from a future filled with unhappiness.

It seemed that, like herself, everyone in the room was holding their breath as she turned her head to Dominic. But even as she turned, with an unexpectedness that had her reeling, he put his arm around her and drew her close against him. But as he did he looked down at her for a fraction of a second, a look that was for her eyes alone, and in that instant she saw an expression of contempt so intense that it was like a knife slashing into her heart. So...she hadn't been mistaken in thinking he would be furious at what she'd done. But she'd have to live with the consequences later. As she dragged her gaze away and saw the expression of growing wonder and joy in Patsy's face...and in Mike's too...she knew, beyond a shadow of a doubt, that she'd done the right thing.

'Angela has beaten me to the punch,' Dominic said, as he held her tightly against him, his arm crushing her ribs, his hand splayed possessively over her hip. Her cheek was pressed against his shoulder, and she could feel the smooth nap of his jacket against her skin, his male scent choking in her nostrils. 'I was just going to make the announcement myself,' he went on ruefully, 'but like most women there are occasions when she loves the limelight, and so she decided to steal the moment from me!'

He laughed, a husky, amused chuckle, and as he did it seemed as if all the breath that everyone had been holding was expelled in one gigantic sigh of relief. The tension dissipated. Laughter filled the room...and it was a happy sound...and with it came a ripple of applause started by Mike. He put his arm around a gleeful Patsy, and, winking at Angela, shook his head as if to say, Well, now, aren't you the dark horse? The only person in the room who wasn't smiling was Starr. The poppy colour had drained from her face, and she was standing there like a ghost; she must have been unsteady, because Max was by her side, supporting her.

'And so,' Dominic continued, 'now that our news is finally out—and, I may add, I am thankful it is, and that Angela and I have finally cleared up the misunderstandings that have kept us apart these last few years— I'd like to propose another toast.' He raised his champagne glass. 'Ladies and gentlemen—to Angela, who has just today promised to be my bride.'

For Angela, the next half-hour passed in a blur. Almost before Dominic had finished his shattering announcement, Patsy had thrust her baby into Mike's arms and rushed over and hugged her with such fervour that Angela felt as if all the breath was being squeezed from her body.

'Oh, how lovely, Angela! We're going to be sisters-in-law! And you have a little boy! Oh, how could you have kept that from me? But I suppose you didn't want Dominic to find out... And when did you and Dominic make up? Was it when you——?'

'That's our secret, Patsy... isn't it, my darling?' As Patsy stepped back, beaming at Angela, Dominic took one of Angela's hands in his, casually, as if it were something he was in the habit of doing often. 'Ask no questions, and you'll be told no lies.'

'Oh, I don't care how it happened, so long as it *has* happened!' Patsy's face became serious. 'It's almost as if you were a fairy godmother with a magic wand, Angela, and you just waved that wand and granted us all our dearest wishes. Everyone's going to get what they want... even Dom, bless his heart. I hope, wherever he is, that he knows...'

'Congratulations, Dominic, darling.' Starr joined their little group, Max by her side. 'It must please you that you'll be taking over the Hall after all. And Mike has just told me he's been writing on the sly for years and has sold a novel—a mystery—to a New York publisher. This really is a day of surprises!'

Starr was taking the whole thing remarkably well, Angela decided, as the older woman, saying, 'Best wishes, little Angela!' stepped forward and embraced her lightly. But as her silver hair brushed Angela's cheek, and her perfume scented the air around them, she whispered in Angela's ear, 'You win, my dear.'

The words were said so softly that Angela wondered if she had imagined them. But when Starr stepped back there was a hardness in her eyes as she flicked them over Angela, a hardness that sent a little chill through her.

Yet, even as Angela tried to make sense of the incident—an incident of which the others must be unaware—Starr was all sweetness and light again.

'I must tell you all,' the ex-actress said with a rippling laugh, 'these two were meant for each other. I've known that from the very beginning—before Dominic knew it himself, I think. When Angela used to play chess with Dom, he always found some excuse to drop by the study.'

Angela felt Dominic's fingers tighten around hers, felt her own quiver in involuntary response. Was it true? Had he really been seeking an excuse just to see her, on those occasions when he'd so casually popped in to say goodnight?

'You're a very perceptive woman, Starr.' Dominic released Angela's hand and slid an arm around her shoulder; she felt his fingers caress the bare skin at her nape, felt a disturbing little tingle shiver down her spine. 'Angela was only fifteen or sixteen then, but already she showed promise of the lovely woman she was to become. What I didn't realise—couldn't have begun to guess— was that the compelling attraction she had for me would eventually evolve into the once-in-a-lifetime kind of love that it has become.'

As he spoke, Angela became aware that the zigzag flashes of light before her eyes—the aura warning her of a migraine—had gone, but in its place had come the headache. A headache brought on by the stress of speaking out, a stress intensified by Starr's incomprehensible whispered comment. '*You win, my dear*'. Win what? But even as she tried to come up with an answer the headache took over. Relentless, agonising, it blotted everything else from her mind, and all other considerations ceased to exist. She winced, and put the heel of her free hand to her head. 'Do you mind?' she said in a weak voice. 'I... I've got a bit of a headache. I need to lie down...'

'I'll take you upstairs.' Patsy frowned anxiously. 'Will an aspirin help?'

'I'm afraid not. If I could just lie down in the dark for a while——'

Patsy uttered a frustrated exclamation as the baby suddenly began crying, a shrill, demanding sound. 'Oh, darn! The timing couldn't have been worse! I'm afraid I'll have to tend to him. Dominic, will you go up with Angela—just get her settled in... maybe a glass of cold water...?'

'Mmm. Excuse us, Starr, Max—keep the party going, won't you? Mike, old chap, how about some more champers for everyone...?'

Angela was thankful for Dominic's supporting arm as she stumbled from the room. She would have been thankful for anyone's arm, actually, but there was something so reassuring about Dominic, despite the hostility vibrating between them. He was the kind of man one would want to have around when one was sick.

Her thoughts seemed to be staggering around in her head, making no sense. When they got to the head of the stairs, Dominic manoeuvred her along the corridor, and made to open the door to the Hyacinth Suite.

'No,' she murmured vaguely. 'I'm in the Daffodil Suite...the same suite Starr gave me last time I was here, the night before Patsy was married.'

She felt Dominic's arm tighten savagely around her waist. 'The Daffodil Suite?'

'Right. At the very end of the corridor. Oh, you know where it is—it's your house, isn't it?'

'It's my house...*now*,' he said curtly, 'but you weren't in the Daffodil Suite last time you were here. Or are you just conveniently forgetting something you don't want to remember? Something you are perhaps ashamed to remember?'

Oh, what was he going on about...? Angela could hardly keep her eyes open as she slid herself from his supporting arm. 'I know where I'm going, Dominic,' she said. 'You can go back now, to the party.'

Despite her headache, she managed to point herself unerringly in the direction of the Daffodil Suite, and had just opened the door when she realised Dominic was right behind her. She was past caring where he was, or what he was thinking, or how confused he was about which suite she had been allocated. The bedroom door was open, she could see the bed, and she made for it with the last remaining vestiges of her strength. A

heartfelt sigh escaped her as she let her limp body fall
heavily on top of the duvet.

'Draw the curtains,' she muttered, and gave herself
up to the pain that was relentlessly boring into her brain.
'Please . . .'

A distant part of her mind was aware of the swish of
drapes being pulled, and blessed darkness blacking out
her vision. In the same part of her mind, she felt her
shoes being slipped off, felt a light cover being placed
gently over her. There was a click as the door
closed . . . and then nothing but the dark, the dryness of
her mouth, the sound of her breathing in the quiet . . .

And the pain.

She must have slept.

When she awoke, she froze for a moment, waiting for
the resumption of the agony in her head . . . but, though
her brain felt as muzzy as if it were stuffed with cotton
wool, the tension had gone, the migraine had passed,
and she drew in a quivering sigh of relief.

But what time was it?

Reaching across to the bedside table, she fumbled for
the light switch. Clicking it on, she glanced at her watch,
and felt a jolt of dismay—it was after five o'clock! She
wrenched herself up to a sitting position, and raked her
hair back from her brow. Not only would the Cranstons
probably be gone, if she didn't hurry, she'd miss the
evening train, at six——

A small sound from over by the window startled her,
and she glanced round. All her thoughts crashed to a
halt as she saw she wasn't alone . . . a man was sitting in
the huge wicker armchair by the hearth, his eyes closed,
his legs crossed comfortably at the knee.

Dominic.

The small sound came again, and she realised it was
a gentle snore. He was sound asleep.

He must have been there all along. When she'd heard
the door closing after he drew the curtains and covered

her, he must have shut it from the inside, and come back into the room, to watch over her.

And as she stared at him, at his face relaxed in sleep, to her dismay she felt the ashes of her long-ago love for him begin to flicker to life once again. All the hurts of the past were forgotten as she saw that, in sleep, his features were as innocent, as vulnerable, as those of a child. And a great sympathy flowed from her to him as she reflected upon the disappointment he must have felt when she had fallen from the pedestal upon which he'd raised her. How sad it was that he could not accept anything less than perfection. Yet now, because of her imperfect self, and her imperfect behaviour, he was going to do what he must have considered the only honourable thing to do, now that her secret was public knowledge...

He was going to make an honest woman of her.

Or so he thought.

There was no way she was going to agree to a marriage of convenience. And the sooner she straightened that out with him the better.

She cleared her throat, loudly, and he opened his eyes. Pushing herself off the bed, she pulled down her pink sweater and tidied the pleats of her knit skirt as she looked at him warily. For the merest fraction of a second, he obviously didn't remember what had happened. He stared at her, sleepily, and as his drowsy gaze roamed over her he smiled. 'Ah, Angela, my love,' he murmured. And then a spasm of pain seemed to cross his face, and with a quick frown he gathered himself together. Clearing his throat as she had done a moment before, he grasped the arms of his chair, and got up. 'Are you feeling better?' His voice was now impassive, with no sign of the tenderness that had been there a moment before.

'Yes, I'm fine now—but if the Cranstons have left I'll have to hurry... The last train...'

'I'll drive you back to Brockton. And please don't argue,' he added. 'You and I have a lot to talk about, plans to make. We can't do it here, where we're likely to be interrupted at any moment.'

He was right; they did have to talk. And she really didn't feel up to arguing. 'Very well,' she said, slipping on her shoes. 'Thank you. When...do you want to leave?'

He looked at his watch. 'We'll go down and have something to eat, then get on our way. OK?'

'OK.'

'And Angela...'

'Yes?'

'For God's sake, try not to look at me as if you're waiting for me to hit you! If we're going to make our marriage work—or at least look as if it's going to work—we've got to convince everybody that we're in love. Could you at least make an effort to——?'

'*Marriage*?' Angela stared disbelievingly at him. 'What marriage? You don't really imagine that I'm going to go through with this farce? I know you only said what you did because you want to be *seen* to be doing the right thing by me, but you must have known I'd not go along with——'

'You have no option.' Dominic's voice had become as iron-hard as a mid-winter frost. 'Now that everyone knows you have a child, the only way to ensure that everyone will believe that child is mine is...for me to marry you. Do you understand?'

With an effort, Angela tried to follow his line of reasoning. 'You mean...you want to prevent anyone looking at the situation and perhaps coming to the conclusion that I'm...*pretending* the child is yours, just so you can inherit the Hall?'

Dominic looked at her, for a long, long moment. His dark eyes were fathomless, so deep that she couldn't even guess what he was thinking. Finally, he said, in a voice that held an edge of mockery, 'Exactly.' He paused before going on steadily, 'Why did you do it, Angela? Why did you speak up? Not for my sake, surely——'

'No,' she said. 'Not for you.'

'For Patsy, then.'

'Yes...mostly for Patsy.'

'You felt you owed her one.'

'Yes, you could say that.'

'"*You could say that*",' he parroted. 'My God, yes, you could certainly say that! But I'm surprised you had the courage. After all, I'd warned you to keep the child a secret. How did you expect I was going to react, upon your melodramatic announcement?'

Angela played nervously with the strap of her watch. 'I...thought perhaps you might tell everyone Nicky wasn't yours. I certainly didn't expect that you'd——'

'Admit to being the child's father? Say I wanted to marry you?'

'You're not going to m——'

'I am going to, Angela. Be sure of that, if you're sure of nothing else. And so when we go downstairs now I want you to act the part of the blushing fiancée——'

'I can't—I won't——'

Her words seemed to act as a challenge. Before she could guess what he was going to do, he'd closed the space between them and taken her in his arms. In the breathless second before she recovered from her shock and opened her mouth to protest, her eyes were filled with a close-up picture of him...of his black hair—rumpled with sleep; his jaw, darkly shadowed; his upper lip, beaded with moisture. And then his mouth was on hers, possessively, relentlessly, and the sweet texture of his flesh moving on hers was so exquisitely sensual that her protest died unuttered. And as his arms tightened around her, and his kiss deepened, the distinctive scent of him filled her nostrils; it was a musky aphrodisiac that stimulated heat in every part of her body, heat that rushed through her veins like a hurtling stream of glowing red lava, heat that hissed across her nerve-endings like a hot silk whip, heat that hummed and throbbed inside her and over her and around her, like a wild creature that wouldn't rest till it found its mate. And she knew Dominic was feeling that heat too, because as she surrendered with a moan to its savage onslaught, putting her arms around his neck and moulding her soft body against his hard, powerful frame, she felt the unmistakable ridge of his desire.

The shock of it sucked the breath from her lungs and at the same moment started her brain functioning again. Pheromones! it shrieked contemptuously—whether contemptuous of nature's secret weapon or contemptuous of her for having been so easily seduced by it Angela wasn't sure. But she didn't wait to find out. Dragging her hands from around Dominic's neck, she clenched them into fists and pushed against his chest with a strength she hadn't known she possessed, and wriggled free of his embrace.

She stepped back, her breath coming raggedly, her cheeks flushed. Challengingly, she stared at him, as if daring him to touch her again . . . but if she had expected him to be the least bit remorseful she was to be disappointed.

'My God, Angela, you should have to wear a sign saying "Danger! Highly flammable!" Touching you is like putting a spark to tinder!' His lips twisted cynically. 'But that's OK, because now you look the way I want my future bride to look—flushed, mussed, and thoroughly bussed. Just make sure you keep that just-been-kissed sparkle in your eyes when we go downstairs . . . at least till you and I are alone again.'

Why did she let this man manipulate her so? One minute she was helpless in his arms, succumbing recklessly to his sexual magnetism . . . the next, she was so infuriated by his arrogance that she could willingly have hired a hit man to annihilate him. But the last thing she wanted was for him to know how easily he could throw her off balance. Cool, calm, poised . . . that was how she wanted to appear.

And that was how she *would* appear!

'Stop playing games, Dominic,' she said. 'And get one thing straight. I'm *not* going to marry you. I'll go on with this little charade till you get things settled with the lawyer regarding the ownership of the Hall. After that, I don't ever want to see you again. I don't want you in my life ... and I don't want you in my son's life either. A boy his age needs a role model and the last person I want him to admire and imitate is you. He needs someone like Mike to look up to—someone who is warm and caring—someone who respects women. Take a leaf out of his book, Dominic—your brother is more of a man that you can ever hope to be.'

For a moment she thought she had gone too far. The skin around his nostrils turned white, and he seemed to be making a tremendous effort not to hit out at her. His hands were clenched tightly, and his eyes had a black, haunted look that sent a chill shivering through her. She'd never really been frightened of him before, but now ...

Deciding she'd better get out while the going was good, Angela moved swiftly to the door and out into the corridor, before he had a chance to stop her. With light, quick steps that echoed the panicky beating of her heart, she ran towards the landing, and then down the stairs. When she got to the bottom, she heard him call after her grimly, 'Come back here; I'm not finished with you yet, you little b——'

But he clipped the words off as the drawing-room door opened, and Angela breathed a shuddering sigh of relief when she saw Patsy come out into the hall. Her friend was accompanied by the Cranstons.

'Oh, there you are, dear!' Maud beamed at her delightedly. 'I was just telling Mike and Patsy that we're going to leave now, and we were hoping you'd be ready to come with us. Are you feeling better?'

'Mmm, I'm fine, thanks,' Angela said breathlessly, 'and I'm ready to leave. I packed my bag earlier—it's at the front door.' Ignoring Dominic, who had joined them at the foot of the stairs, she gave Patsy a warm hug. 'It's been *lovely* seeing you again. Thanks so much for inviting me.'

'You must come back again soon.' Patsy beamed at her. 'And bring Dominic junior—I can't want to meet him.'

Mike appeared, and some malicious devil inside Angela made her move across to him and give him a hug as warm as the one she had just given Patsy.

'It's been super seeing you again, Mike,' she said. 'Brought back so many happy memories.'

'Super seeing you too, love,' Mike said with a big grin. 'And delighted you're to be one of the family. Looking forward to seeing a lot more of you in the future.'

She had hugged Mike to annoy Dominic, and she'd succeeded. As she turned away she caught a glimpse of his face, and she had never seen such burning rage in anyone's eyes before. She felt a sense of smug satisfaction; he wasn't always going to get his own way, not if she could help it. He had been trying to keep her away from Mike for the past two days, but at last she'd been able to thwart him. It felt good.

In a flurry of goodbyes, she went to get her bag, but Dominic beat her to it.

'Is this it?' he asked in low, glacial tones, pointing to her canvas holdall.

'Yes,' she muttered, bending to pick it up. 'But I can manage it myself.'

'What will people think if I let my bride-to-be carry her own luggage?' he retorted under his breath as he firmly removed her hand from the leather handle. In a loud, hearty voice he said, 'Here, darling, let me carry that for you. Can't have you straining that lovely slender arm!'

'Bastard!' she hissed, somehow managing to curve her lips into a smile as they passed Mike and Patsy, who had gone outside with the Cranstons, and were sitting on a low wall at the top of the front steps.

Dominic cupped her elbow in a steely grip as they crossed the gravelled forecourt to the Cranstons' car. Harry had opened the back door of the Volvo, and Dominic thrust Angela's bag inside.

As she made to get in, he said, 'I can't get away till the end of the week.' His voice was pleasant but his fingers bit cruelly into her flesh. 'Phone me tonight when you get home. We'll start making plans for the wedding.'

As he spoke, Dominic pulled her close. His kiss might have looked harmless to the others, but it was far from harmless. It was instead a deep and arrogant violation, his tongue sliding with insolent sensuality between her parted lips. 'There,' he said in a light tone as he released her. 'That's just to remind you I'll never let you go again.'

She heard Harry chuckle as she slid into her seat. 'There's a man who knows his own mind,' he grinned as he pulled the car away. 'And a man with a mind of his own!'

Yes, Angela thought furiously as she stared out of the window and tried without success to control the stormy feelings raging inside her, he knows his own mind, and he has a mind of his own.

But she, too, knew her own mind and had a mind of her own. And no one, not even someone as strong-willed and powerful as Dominic Elliot, could force her to marry him against her wishes. She had no intention of phoning him that night, as he'd commanded…or any other night.

She had no intention of ever seeing him again.

CHAPTER SEVEN

'JUST let me off at the next corner,' Angela said to Harry Cranston. 'Our lane's one-way so you won't be able to drive back up it, and everyone gets lost when they try to find the return route to the main road.'

'Harry always gets lost.' Maud's diamond earrings glinted as she turned to Angela with a chuckle. 'So we'll take your advice, dear. Here we are—Hawthorne Lane. Pull in by that lamp-post, Harry.'

Angela thanked the couple once again, and stood on the pavement, waving, as the Volvo swung out on to the road and back into the stream of traffic. It had been a pleasant drive back, Maud's friendly chatter helping to pass the time...and helping to keep her mind off Dominic.

But now, as she walked slowly along the lane, her overnight bag in one hand, she found him pushing his way relentlessly into her thoughts again.

Dusk had fallen, the streetlights were on, and the smell of nightstock from the gardens on either side of her scented the still warm evening air. It was, she realised, a night very like that night by the lake, when she and Dominic had made love. A night made for romance.

Well, there was no room in her life now for romance. No room for a man. Even her father had let her down. That had been a shock, the way he'd accepted Dominic— no, more than accepted him. He'd made him welcome in his home, had warmly invited him to return.

And it hadn't taken Dominic long to take advantage of the generously proffered hospitality. He had already invited himself back this coming weekend. She would have to have a talk with her father, let him know that, as far as she was concerned, Dominic was not welcome at Hawthorne Cottage.

The white picket gate clicked quietly behind her as she walked up the path. The living-room—to the right of the front door—was in darkness, but the kitchen, to the left, was brightly lit up, the curtains open, and she saw her father there, at the sink. Molly was with him.

Graeme was washing the dishes, Molly drying them . . . and they were talking. Angela could hear the sound of their voices through the half-open window. Molly was looking up at Graeme earnestly, and as Angela began walking up the front steps she heard her father's voice, clearly, in the hushed evening air.

'This is Angela's home, love, but she'd not stay here, no matter how hard I tried to persuade her, if you and I were married. I know my Angie—she'd feel as if she was in the way. And if she didn't have me to look after Nicky for her she'd be in a real bind. She depends on me——'

'Graeme, Angela's twenty-three—surely she's old enough to take charge of her own life? She's healthy, she has a good job now, and there are some nice little flats not too far from her place of work, with quite reasonable rents.'

'I know, love, I know. But she has no savings—she's been putting every spare penny towards paying off her student loan—and there's no way she can afford to rent a flat at present, no matter how reasonable the rent, and also pay someone to care for Nicky while she's at work. Besides, you know she doesn't feel happy leaving him with anyone except me. . .and I wouldn't be happy about it either . . .'

Molly's deep sigh brought his words to a trailing halt. 'Oh, Graeme, I do understand . . . and you know how fond I am of Angela. But all I'm thinking about is *you*, and your health. I agreed to keep your heart condition a secret from her—though I must admit I panicked yesterday and phoned her——'

'I told you not to worry about that, love. You did the right thing—after all, you thought I was going to kick the bucket!'

'Oh, Graeme, don't talk like that. I did think you were having a major heart attack, though——'

'Just indigestion, love!'

'I know—but it *could* have been a heart attack. The doctor has said over and over again that stress is the very worst thing for you and you *must* avoid it. Looking after Nicky is just too much for you.'

'I love the lad, Moll——'

'That's not the point,' Molly said tearfully. 'Graeme, you've spent the last few years looking after Angela and her son . . . now you're the one who needs looking after. I'm just waiting for you to say the word.'

Angela felt waves of shock ripple through her—shock and horror, and dismay. For a long, mindless moment she just stood there, feeling as if her whole world was dissolving under her feet like quicksand. Finally, barely aware of what she was doing, she turned to her right and stumbled along the garden path that led around the cottage to the back door. Once there, she paused, her breath coming in painful gasps as she leaned against the wall.

Her dad . . . and Molly.

Why had she never noticed there was something going on between them? Even when Patsy had asked if the two were involved in a relationship she had airily laughed away the suggestion.

And more shocking—much more shocking—was the discovery that her father had a heart problem.

They wanted to get married—Molly wanted to look after Graeme. And she, Angela, was standing in the way.

She had been so busy with her own life, and Nicky's, that she had never stopped to ask herself if she was taking advantage of her father. He had always seemed so happy to have them living with him, so delighted to do the housework, so proud to look after Nicky, to take him grocery shopping with him, to take him to the park on a Saturday morning, to take him to the barber when he needed a haircut...

To do all the things that had made her own life easier.

Shame and remorse were like lead weights on her heart as she tried to gather herself together. She must never let her father or Molly know she'd overheard their conversation. But somehow, some way, she must take from her father the burden she had so unthinkingly bestowed on him, and let him have a life of his own.

Taking in a deep breath, she opened the back door.

The passage was in darkness, but as she came to Nicky's room she saw that his night light was on. He was sound asleep, his arms loosely around his beloved Maggie, the stuffed bulldog—now one-eyed and threadbare—which her father had given him when he was a baby. Like a shadow, she slipped across the room, and tidied the rumpled covers before sitting down on the edge of the bed. As she slumped there, blurred eyes fixed on the little boy who was her whole world, she asked herself distraughtly what she was going to do. She would, of course, have to move out. But how was she going to manage when she did? The meagreness of her bank account was, naturally, a major cause for worry, but the fact that her father would no longer be available to babysit Nicky was a much more distressing aspect of her situation. She felt a fluttering panic knot her stomach as she visualised the problem of trying to find someone to replace him, someone she could trust implicitly, someone who would give Nicky the loving care he deserved.

But sitting there was going to solve nothing. With a sigh, she brushed a lingering kiss on Nicky's brow, and then, smoothing his blond hair tenderly, got up. She grimaced as the mattress creaked, but he didn't waken, and she tiptoed from the room and closed the door quietly behind her.

She was aware that her breathing was quick and shallow. Inhaling deeply, she tried to regulate it as she made her way along the hallway, noticing in a distant corner of her mind that the aroma of some spicy Italian dish lingered in the air—probably lasagne, one of her father's specialities.

'Anyone home?' she called softly as she approached the open doorway. 'Dad? Are you there?'

Had she not overheard their conversation earlier she would never have suspected anything was wrong. Her father greeted her with his usual enthusiastic hug, and Molly's greeting also was warm and sincere. The two could have won Oscars for their acting, Angela thought unhappily.

'It's late, lass,' Graeme said, glancing at the white clock on the wall. 'Was your train held up?'

'No, Dad.' Angela slipped off her jacket and draped it over one of the ladder-back chairs set around the table. 'I . . . missed the train, and got a drive back from friends of the Elliotts' who were at the christening.'

'That was handy, dear.' Molly looked around the kitchen, and went on, 'Well, I think that's everything tidied away, Graeme, so I'll get along home.'

'All right, Moll. I'll see you to the door.'

'Just a sec, before you go, Molly—I have something to tell you both.' Angela smiled, though her vision had again become blurred; she hoped with all her heart that Molly and her father would think the tears swimming in her eyes were tears of joy. 'When I was at the Hall, Dominic and I had a long talk. We've cleared up all the misunderstandings between us—and this morning he asked me to marry him.' Her voice trembled, as did her hands, which she had clasped together in front of her, at her waist. 'I accepted his proposal. I've never been happier in my life. I just can't wait to become Dominic's wife.'

Impulsive. She had always been impulsive. When was she going to learn?

As she came downstairs next morning, dressed for work, Angela asked herself for the thousandth time the question that had kept her awake half the night: what on earth had impelled her to blurt out those dreadful lies?

But of course she knew the answer. It had seemed like the perfect solution to the problem facing her—she would tell her father she was going to marry Dominic, and her father would then feel free to marry Molly. Dominic was going to be a complication, of course, because he was determined to get her to the altar, but she would just keep putting him off, keep making excuses as to why she couldn't set a wedding date. Then, after her dad and Molly had been married for a few weeks, and she had got her own life reorganised, she would break off with him altogether. In all probability, he would be relieved—after all, the only reason he had made the announcement of their wedding was to confirm to everyone that Nicky was his. If the plans for a wedding fell flat, people would just think they had had another tiff.

Downstairs, she found her father standing by the stove in his ragged old brown and beige checked dressing-gown, stirring a pot of porridge. The sight of his familiar figure, the smell of the porridge and perking coffee, the cosiness of the homely kitchen, made Angela think of the hundreds of other mornings when she'd come down to this warm, reassuring comfort. She'd always taken it for granted . . . and had never, till today, asked herself if her father was content with his life.

'Dad.' She walked over to him and, putting her arms round him, leaned her head on his shoulder. 'Have I ever told you how much I love you?'

'Aye, lass.' There was a smile in his voice. 'That you have. Many times, and in many ways.' He patted her head. 'And I love you too.' He chuckled. 'And so, it seems, does someone else. Here——' he turned away and lifted a copy of *The Times* from the table behind him '—have a look at this!'

Angela took the paper. It was opened at the 'hatches, matches, and despatches'... and, as she frowningly glanced over the small print, she murmured, 'What am I supposed to be looking for, Dad?'

'There!' Her father's index finger stabbed an announcement at the top of the page, under a society news heading. 'That man of yours doesn't waste much time, does he?'

An engagement has been announced between Dominic Elliott of Hadleigh Hall, Hadleigh, Norfolk, and Angela Jane Fairfax of Hawthorne Cottage, Brockton, Sussex. The wedding will take place on October the first in the private chapel at Hadleigh Hall...

There was more but Angela didn't read it. Couldn't read it. Her eyes refused to focus, her thoughts were so scattered that she just couldn't get them to make sense. Vaguely she was aware of her father saying something about, 'He's in an almighty rush, isn't he? Not about to let you slip away a second time. Oh, Angela, love, I couldn't be happier for you...'

Trapped.

The word echoed around and around in her head. She was well and truly trapped. That Dominic had announced their engagement in a national newspaper would have been bad enough... but he had gone further. Oh, so much further. He had, of his own accord, set the date for their wedding—her stomach seemed to turn right over as her eyes became frozen on the date, a mere three weeks away—without even so much as consulting her... and now, to all intents and purposes, it was set in stone. Had he announced a date six months from now she could have made sure her father and Molly were safely married by that time, and with a bit of luck she herself would have had her own life in order, financially and otherwise, and she could have slipped out of the engagement at the last minute without giving her father any cause to worry about her. But with the day only three weeks away...

Of course she could tell Dominic she wanted to put it off. But wouldn't her father suspect something if she did? Hadn't she told him last night she'd never been happier, and hadn't she told him also, in *ecstatic* tones, that she couldn't *wait* to be Dominic's wife?

The sound of the phone ringing barely punctuated her consciousness. Her father answered it, and, through a mist of confusion, she realised he was talking to Dominic.

'Ah, good morning, my good man,' he was saying. 'Yes, we do subscribe to *The Times*—one of the little luxuries I've allowed myself since I retired! Let me congratulate you, and wish you all the happiness in the world. I must say, you've made a grand choice. Our Angie's a gem.' There was a pause, while he listened, and then he said gruffly, 'Aye, lad, I know you will. Here, I'll let you talk to her. Lucky you called just now— she's just going to have breakfast and then she'll be leaving for work. Here, Angela, it's for you.'

Angela moved her features into what she prayed would pass for an eager smile. 'Thanks, Dad.' Her palms had become damp with perspiration, and before taking the receiver from him she wiped them on the seat of her jeans.

'I'll go through and see if Nicky's awake yet...' her father picked up his coffee-mug '...and leave you two love-birds alone.' Eyes twinkling, he crossed the kitchen, closing the door behind him as he left.

Angela drew in a deep breath, and let it out again in a shudder. She caught a glimpse of her reflection in the chrome surface of the toaster and was appalled at the grey pallor of her face. It had looked exactly like that, she remembered, the day Dominic had jilted her. She cleared her throat as tears threatened to well up, and took a minute to gather herself together. When she finally said 'Hello?' her voice came out coolly, steadily.

'Ah. Good morning, darling.' There was no mistaking the snide sexual innuendo in Dominic's tone. 'The first of many mornings, I hope, when I shall be able to say that to you before you've eaten breakfast.'

'Good morning, Dominic.' Don't let him bait you, she warned herself. Just say what you have to say, and say it firmly. 'You had no right to fix a wedding date without consulting me. What you've done is——'

'What I've done, my darling, is forestall any devious stone-walling tactics on your part. I've given you three weeks to prepare yourself for the wedding and for the changes you'll have to make in your life. It gives you ample time to give notice at your job, ample time to purchase a trousseau——'

'I have no intention of purchasing a trousseau,' Angela said curtly. 'For one thing, I don't have the money, and, for another, the last thing I want to do is dress to please you. This marriage is going to be a sham.'

There was a long, long silence at the other end of the line. The only sound in the kitchen was the slow, steady drip of water in the sink. The tap needed a washer, Angela thought abstractedly. Her father had said he'd fix it this week some time. Nicky had told him he wanted to watch, wanted to learn how to——

Oh, God, she was going crazy. With an effort, Angela dragged her thoughts to the present. Why was Dominic not answering? What was he thinking? Was he——?

'So,' his voice was taut, the lazy drawl of a moment ago gone, 'you agree...there *will* be a wedding?'

Angela dragged a weary hand through her hair. 'Yes,' she said, 'there will be a wedding.'

Again there was a pause, but this time a shorter one. 'You surprise me, Angela.' If he was surprised, his tone didn't reveal it. In fact, it revealed no emotion whatsoever. 'I had expected a battle.'

Yes, he would have expected a battle. After the way she'd acted yesterday, he would indeed have expected a battle. The reason there wasn't going to be one was none of his business. 'No, Dominic,' she said, 'no battle. But don't think, because of that, that you will have things your own way——'

'I'll come to Brockton on Friday and we can talk——'

'No,' she said tersely, 'you won't come here on Friday. I don't want to see you before the day of our wedding. And I'll tell you right now, over the phone, the way I want things to be. I want it to be a very quiet ceremony, with the only guests being Starr, Patsy, Mike and Patsy's mother on your side—Max, too, if he's still there—and Nicky, my father and Molly on mine. There will be no honeymoon, and there will be no physical contact between the two of us when we're alone. These are my terms. Take them or leave them.'

'My, my, my!' Dominic's mocking laugh was threaded with admiration. 'You have come a long way in five years, Angela! Whatever happened to the shy, sweet girl I once knew?'

Angela's hand tightened on the telephone. Had she been shy and sweet? Her lips twisted bitterly. Yes, she had, in days gone by, been shy and sweet. She had also been young, vulnerable, innocent...and trusting. But those days were long past, and they would never come again.

'You, Dominic,' she said in a hard voice, '*you* are what happened to that shy, sweet girl.' And, knowing she shouldn't, knowing it would reveal to him how he had upset her, she thumped the receiver back into place with a resounding crash and cut him off.

As soon as she got to work that morning, she handed in her notice. Her supervisor, Mabel Gunn, seemed a bit put out to hear she'd be leaving at the end of the month, especially since it wasn't too long ago that she'd been hired. But when the older woman discovered the reason her attitude changed in a flash.

'You're to be married? How *wonderful*,' she enthused, putting down the potted palm she was carrying and hugging Angela. 'You must be absolutely over the moon!'

Over the moon was not exactly how she would have described the way she felt, Angela thought. Distraught, frustrated, angry, resentful—those words would surely have better reflected her state of mind. And how very difficult it was to hide those emotions from other people...

Especially from her father. She knew it was absolutely essential that she keep up her happy, light-hearted act when she was with him, but it was a dreadful strain.

That night, as they sat in the living-room after Nicky was in bed, she glanced over at him and found that, though he had the TV on, he was looking not at the screen, but at her, and there was a gleam of excitement in his eyes. It had been there ever since he'd shown her the announcement in *The Times*...and she knew he must be expecting to see the same kind of gleam in hers.

'Angie, love——' he clicked off the TV and leaned forward '—I have something I want to say to you.'

Angela hid a sigh. Surely he wasn't going to launch into a father-and-daughter talk, now that she was on the brink of marriage? It was a little late for that, she reflected wryly, as she looked at the framed photo of Nicky on the mantelpiece. They should have had such a talk when she was a teenager—*before* she gave her heart...and her virginity!...to Dominic. But would she have listened? Probably not.

He went on, frowning now, 'You told me this morning that you want a small wedding. Now, I have no problem with that—that's your decision to make. What I do have a problem with is your insisting you're going to wear that green dress you've worn to every social occasion since Nicky was born. Oh——' he put up a hand to stop her automatic protest '—I know you've never had money to fritter on fancy clothes, and I admire you for your thrifty ways, just as I admire you for always putting Nicky's needs before your own. But Angie, be your wedding small, as you wish it, or the largest, most extravagant affair you could imagine, the memory of that day is going to be with you... and with your husband... for the rest of your lives.'

He got up from his chair, and, lifting the silver lid from the antique biscuit barrel on the mantelpiece, he took out a folded piece of paper. 'That memory is going to be with me, too, love. And while I listen to you and Dominic making your solemn promises to each other I'll be thinking of your mother.' There was a catch in his voice. 'She wouldn't have wanted you to marry in an old dress, Angela. She'd have wanted you to wear something very special.'

He opened out the piece of paper—Angela saw now that it was a cheque. 'This is for you, for your wedding-day. I've been putting aside a little each month ever since I retired. A dowry, if you will. So please an old man——' his hand trembled as he handed Angela the cheque '—and give him a memory to cherish.'

Reluctantly, Angela took the cheque, and when she saw the amount he'd written there she almost cried out. How he must have scrimped, to have been able to put by so much. And how could she refuse it? She couldn't be so cruel.

'Oh, Dad...' She rose from her chair and wrapped her arms around his slight body, her cheek pressed against the rough flannel of his shirt, against his heart, the heart she knew now was frail and unreliable. 'Thank you,' she whispered. 'Thank you so very much. What can I ever do to repay you for all the kindness and loving you've given me?'

'The only thing I want you to do,' he said gruffly, 'is to buy yourself a new dress.'

'I will, Dad...but it won't be white—it can't be white.' Her laugh was tremulous. She pulled away from him, and rubbed her fingertips over her eyes, brushing away the tears.

'No.' His eyes smiled into hers. 'No, not white. What colour does that young man of yours like you to wear? *That's* the colour you should wear on your wedding-day.'

The very last thing she wanted to do was think of her wedding-day. It loomed ahead, like a huge crouching monster, just waiting to snap her up in its horrid jaws. She just couldn't cope with it.

Yet as her father stood waiting for her answer, his face bright with interest and anticipation, she felt her heart give an anxious little flutter. If she didn't play her part better—the part of the impatient and enraptured fiancée—surely he would begin to suspect something was wrong. If that happened, instead of ensuring his happiness she might actually destroy it...and, with it, his already precarious health.

'Red,' she said lightly, 'Dominic likes me in red.' She desperately hoped that no sign of her unhappiness showed in her voice or in her expression.

Her father scratched his head, and then he grinned. 'Then, lass,' he said stoutly, 'red it shall be. That might not be the colour most folks would choose for a wedding dress, but then you don't have to worry about "most folks", do you?' Lovingly, he put an arm around her shoulder. 'The only one *you* want to please is Dominic.'

As Angela stood leaning against him, out of nowhere an old saying came into her mind, one that she'd seen in a magazine many years before:

> Marry in red,
> You're better off dead.

Was that how she was going to feel, married to Dominic?

CHAPTER EIGHT

AUTUMN mist, gauzy and silver-grey, floated over Hadleigh Hall's green lawns and wreathed the bronze and crimson leaves of its stately oaks on the day of the wedding.

The Elliott family's private chapel was situated about a mile from the estate's entrance gates, and as Angela looked out of the car window at the beautiful park through which she was being driven she found her thoughts straying to her last phone conversation with Dominic, which had taken place the week before. It was the fourth time he'd called since the day she'd agreed to marry him.

'I'll see you in the chapel,' she had said to him in a clipped voice. 'And please *don't* call me again. I have nothing more to say to you.'

'In that case,' Dominic had retorted in an equally curt tone, 'I shall certainly not call again. But tell me,' he went on sarcastically, 'how are you planning to get here? Are you all four coming by train, in your wedding finery?'

'As a matter of fact, we are,' Angela said stiffly. 'And we'll get a taxi from the station to the chapel. There's a train that will get us there in good——'

'You have laid down certain conditions for this marriage,' Dominic's voice came harshly over the line, 'conditions which I have accepted. Now I'm going to lay down one of my own. You will not, I repeat not, come to our wedding courtesy of British Rail. I'll send a car for you.' He gave a grim laugh. 'I'd come and pick you up myself, were it not unlucky for the groom to set eyes on his bride before the wedding... I think we have enough

119

strikes against us as it is, without tempting fate in that way. Can you be ready by noon?'

Angela realised she had twisted the telephone cord into a knot and, with an effort, she stilled her nervous fingers. But as she weighed Dominic's offer she admitted to herself that there was really only one response she could make. The prospect of subjecting her father to a long train journey and a taxi ride, in addition to the stress and excitement of the wedding, had been gnawing away at her for days. If she were going on her own, she'd have turned down Dominic's offer out of hand, but...

'Yes,' she said. 'We'll be ready by noon. Thank you.'

'So...' For a moment there was silence at the other end of the line. Then Dominic went on, 'That's it, then. Do you have any questions?'

'Only one.' For no one but her father would Angela have humbled herself to ask Dominic for a favour. 'Will your driver take Molly and Dad back to Brockton after it's all over?'

'Would you like them to stay the night?'

'No... thank you. I know they'll want to get home.'

'In that case, of course I'll arrange for them to be driven back. But be sure to let me know if they change their minds. The Hall will be your home as from to-morrow. Your family and friends will always be welcome.'

His words had a sincere ring to them. All of a sudden, with no warning, Angela felt tears prick the back of her eyes. Oh, if only the last five years had never happened. If only—instead of shunning her—Dominic had spoken those reassuring words to her when he'd come home from abroad on the morning of Patsy's wedding; if only...

If only.

Two of the most poignant words in the English language.

Afraid to speak, in case Dominic would hear the regret and sadness in her voice, Angela slowly took the phone from her ear without saying goodbye, and hung up.

She hadn't heard from him since.

Today his driver had arrived at Hawthorne Cottage promptly at noon. Molly had come over about fifteen minutes before, looking lovely in a pale blue suit and a matching hat with a dainty feather, and Angela, watching from the living-room window, had felt a lump swell in her throat as she saw her father walk down the garden path to meet her. He perhaps guessed she was watching, for he didn't kiss Molly, but whatever he said brought a soft glow to the older woman's face. His own face, as they walked up the path together, held a look of such happiness, such contentment that any doubts that she was doing the right thing fled from Angela's mind.

'Are we nearly there?' Nicky, sitting in the front between his mother and the chauffeur, addressed his question to Angela and brought her mind swiftly back to the present.

'Yes, Nicky. The chapel's just beyond that huge oak tree.'

'Then I'll see Dominic again.' He turned towards the driver, a middle-aged man who wore a navy uniform and peaked hat. 'I'm Dominic too,' he informed him proudly. 'And I'm going to live here with my mother and father. I'm going to be Dominic Elliott the seventh.'

Angela saw the corner of the driver's mouth twitch. 'Well, that's quite a mouthful,' he said. 'Now, laddie, if you just look out that window, you'll see the chapel.' He glanced briefly at his watch. 'The rest of the wedding party will be inside waiting, ma'am. We're about ten minutes late, but——' this time his smile was a wide one '—every bride is entitled to keep her groom waiting.' With a skilful sweep of the steering-wheel, he drew the limousine to a halt right in front of the chapel steps. 'Especially——' he turned to Angela '—when the bride is as lovely as you. If you'll pardon my boldness, you look prettier than the picture on a chocolate box. That velvet dress is something else...and I've never seen a bride wear scarlet before. Just wait till I tell the missus.

And Mr Elliott . . . why, when he sees you, his eyes are going to pop clean out of his head.'

'Is he talking about Dominic, Mummy?' Nicky looked aghast as he stared up at his mother. 'His eyes are going to pop out of his head when he sees you? Is he going to *die*?'

The chauffeur gave a bark of laughter, and Angela found herself joining in . . . heard her father and Molly chuckling too. She gave Nicky a comforting hug and said, 'Of course not, you little goose, it's just a way of speaking. It means he's going to get a . . . big surprise, that's all.'

The little incident somehow, miraculously, broke the tension that had been tightening inside Angela ever since she'd awakened that morning. So much so that when Mike, looking smart in a beautifully cut charcoal-grey suit, appeared from inside the chapel and started down the steps towards the car, a welcoming smile on his face, she was able to return that smile in a genuine, natural way.

He helped her out of the vehicle and, holding her away from him, looked her up and down admiringly. 'My God, you look fantastic, Angela! You must be the first Elliott bride to come to the altar in scarlet! There must be a few Elliott women turning in their graves right now.'

'I don't know whether I should take that as a compliment or not . . . but thanks, anyway! You're looking pretty snazzy yourself, Mike.'

He grinned. 'A well-cut suit can hide a multitude of sins—including the extra weight I've put on in the last few years!'

'All the more of you for Patsy to cuddle,' Angela chuckled, and then, as the others joined them, she said, 'Now let me introduce everyone.'

After all the introductions were over, Mike tucked one of Molly's arms in his, and said, 'I'll take Nicky and Molly in—Nicky, hold Molly's hand so you don't get lost!—I'll get them seated, and then I'll go and take my place with Dominic. When the organist starts playing the *Bridal March*, Graeme, that's your cue to bring Angela up the aisle. Angela, it's too bad you couldn't have come last night; we could have had a run-through——'

'Mike, you don't have to worry.' She threw him a reassuring smile. 'Dominic went over everything with me on the phone last week. It's going to be a simple ceremony—there was no need for a rehearsal.' Bending down, she gave Nicky a quick kiss. 'Be good, darling, and don't talk once you're inside. Do everything Molly tells you.'

'I will, Mummy.'

As she watched them disappear into the chapel, her father held out her bouquet, a charming nosegay of sweet-scented white roses and delicate fern which had been a gift from Mabel, her supervisor at work. 'Your flowers, love.'

'Thanks, Dad.' Angela smiled ruefully as she took the bouquet. 'I've *really* done things backwards, haven't I? Most women dream of having a white wedding and red roses——'

'And you're having a red wedding and white roses.' Her father put an arm round her. 'It doesn't matter, love, what the colour is or what the order is. The promises you're going to make—those are what matter. You've chosen to make them in a house of God, Angela, and I'm glad you have. Put all your heart into your promises, and all your soul, because those vows, once made, are forever.'

The strains of the *Bridal March* wafted through the open doorway as if on cue. Angela knew she had never needed her father's support as much as she needed it now. Her hand trembled as she placed it on his arm, her legs trembled as she walked from the misty afternoon into the shadows of the small narthex.

And her heart trembled as she caught sight of Dominic, standing at the altar.

He had half turned, to watch her approach. She knew there were others in the sanctuary, but Dominic was the only one she saw, and, even though they were separated by the length of the aisle, his physical impact slammed into her, tearing the breath from her lungs as if she'd walked into the blast of a hurricane.

Like Mike, he was wearing a dark suit, but, unlike Mike, he had absolutely nothing to hide, his superbly cut clothing only serving to accentuate the magnificence of his tall, muscular frame. The single-breasted jacket draped his shoulders in a way that brought a strange tightness to Angela's throat; the narrow-fitting trousers outlined his powerful thighs in a way that caused an equally queer twisting in the pit of her stomach. If there was anything sinful about this man's body—Angela suddenly felt so light-headed that she thought she might faint—it was that it was so flagrantly male, and so *dev-astatingly* sexy.

She saw his gaze slide over her, saw his eyelids flicker, his Adam's apple jerk convulsively as he took in her scarlet dress.

It was, she knew, a beautiful garment. Of silk velvet, it had a low neckline that revealed her creamy skin, a fitted bodice that clung to her softly rounded breasts, a straight skirt that accentuated her waist and hips. When she'd tried it on in Harrods she'd acknowledged, without the faintest trace of conceit, that she looked wonderful in it. Elegant, sophisticated, mature...

And desirable.

When Dominic Elliott saw her in it, she had mused with a grim smile as she'd scrutinised her reflection in the changing-room mirror, he would get a glimpse of just what he'd lost five years ago. And what he could never hope to have now.

As she walked the last steps along the aisle to join him, she was intensely conscious of his perusal...a perusal that seemed to go on forever. And when he finally raised his eyes to meet hers she was rocked by a jolt of shock. In the clear green depths was a look of sorrow, of unhappiness, so profound that she felt as if an arrow had pierced her heart. And the triumph which she'd expected to feel didn't materialise; what she felt, instead, was regret. Regret at having played such a childish, taunting game.

Throat muscles tight, she dragged her gaze away from him as she took her stance in front of the minister.

Vaguely she heard the elderly man ask, 'Who giveth this Woman...?' and vaguely she heard her father answer before he drew away. Nervously she cleared her throat, and then wished she hadn't—the noise seemed so loud, now that the organist had stopped playing and the echoes of the music had faded away.

The minister started speaking, but the words were just a pattern of sounds. No matter how she tried, she couldn't concentrate—couldn't concentrate on what he was saying because of Dominic's closeness. He wasn't touching her, but she could feel the impact of his presence on every nerve-ending. It was almost as if what was happening was a dream. A dream in which she was participating, yet a dream she seemed not to be part of.

But she had to be part of it.

The minister was saying, 'I, Angela...'

She found herself thinking of what her father had said outside the chapel, just moments ago. *'Put all your heart into your promises... because those vows, once made, are forever'.*

She knew she could no longer avoid looking at Dominic, and, taking in a deep breath, she turned and raised her gaze to his—and surprised a look of such tenderness that she almost cried out. A moment later, it was gone, and his expression was shuttered, closing her out... but it was too late. Though it had only lasted for the space of a heartbeat, she had captured a glimpse of the Dominic she had once known.

And it was to that man she spoke, when she uttered her solemn vows, the same vows he had just made to her.

'I, Angela, take thee, Dominic, to my wedded husband . . . to love, cherish, and to obey . . .'

Green eyes looked into hers, with such intensity that she felt her heart give a painful twist. And then the gold band, still warm from Mike's palm, was being slipped on her finger. Flesh touched flesh, briefly . . .

'I now pronounce that they be Man and Wife together . . .'

As the minister's words echoed in the small chapel, Angela felt Dominic's hands on her shoulders, pulling her towards him. She heard him draw in a sharp breath, and then his arms were around her, in a hard embrace.

In the split-second before he kissed her, their eyes met, and, to her amazement, she saw that his were misted. Misted . . . with *tears*? Surely not! Surely the cold, arrogant Dominic she had agreed to marry hadn't been *moved* by the ceremony? She must be mistaken . . .

A moment later, he was kissing her, and everything else was forgotten; all she knew was the taste and feel and intent of him. Mint-fresh lips, warm sensual skin, demanding pressure. The kiss was over almost before it started, but it left her feeling weak and breathless, as if he'd been holding her underwater. And even after he had released her she could feel the taste of him on her mouth . . . and the smooth texture of his jacket seemed still imprinted on her own fingertips, the intangible proof that when he had kissed her she had put her arms around him. She could have sworn she hadn't moved.

It wasn't till she was in the drawing-room of the Hall, a glass of champagne in her hand, and everyone chattering happily around Dominic and herself, showering good wishes upon them, that she began to lose the dizzy feeling that had assailed her when Dominic had kissed her. Cold reality hit when Mike asked Dominic if he could kiss the bride.

Dominic's arm had been casually around her waist; now she felt it tighten, so fiercely that for a moment she felt short of breath. But when he spoke it was with an ease which belied the force of his possessive grip. 'Yes, little brother, you may kiss my bride.'

Angela was barely aware of Mike's friendly kiss, as she tried to come up with a reason for Dominic's unexpected tension. It wasn't the first time, she realised, that he'd acted that way—he'd done the same thing when Mike had greeted her on his return from the city with Starr the day before the christening.

And into her head all at once slid the memory of how Dominic had, smoothly but firmly, interrupted Mike that same evening when he'd attempted to reminisce with her about the past; how he had, just as smoothly and just as firmly, prevented Mike from joining her when she'd announced she was going for a walk to clear her headache. He, Dominic, had then announced arrogantly that *he* would accompany her.

Was he, for some reason, trying to exert some authority over Mike? She had always thought the two got along—got along very well, in fact. Had something happened to destroy the close relationship that had existed between them? If so, she decided with a feeling of confusion, the restraint was all on Dominic's part; she had noticed no coolness or reticence on——

'Excuse us, won't you, Mike?' Dominic's voice broke into her thoughts. 'I'd like a word with Angela—alone—before we go through for our meal.'

'Sure.' Mike grinned. 'But don't keep her to yourself too long.' Whistling the *Bridal March* cheerfully under his breath, he turned to join the others.

Dominic was doing it again, Angela thought with a feeling of bewilderment—keeping her away from Mike. But before she could even try to figure out the reason Dominic had manoeuvred her across to one of the huge bay windows.

'It's customary for the groom to give his bride a present on her wedding-day.' His eyes were unreadable as, looking down at her, he withdrew a tiny velvet-covered box from his jacket pocket and opened it; inside was a stunningly beautiful antique ruby ring. 'It was my grandmother's,' he said, lifting the ring from its satin bed. 'I want you to have it.'

Angela's hand felt cold as he lifted it, cold and limp. She had painted her almond-shaped fingernails scarlet the night before, exactly the same colour as her dress. As he slipped the ring on her finger, beside the plain gold band he'd placed there earlier, she felt her throat tighten. If only... If only...

'You have nothing to say?' Dominic demanded, after a moment.

'Whatever I say is only going to sound clichéd,' she answered in a quiet voice. 'And in the circumstances I don't know why you think it necessary to give me an engagement ring.'

'There's no point in leaving this one lying in a box where no one can see it. Since this is going to be my first, last, and only marriage, you may as well have it.'

His careless shrug said more than any words, but Angela could read into it what he meant. It wasn't that he particularly wanted *her* to wear it... he just thought somebody should.

'It matches your dress, doesn't it?' he drawled. 'It's almost as if I'd guessed what colour you were going to wear.' As he spoke, still holding her hand, he ran a finger along the yoke of the dress, his fingers teasing the skin over her collarbone. 'Why did you choose scarlet, Angela? Did you want to turn me on as you walked down the aisle?'

'Of course I didn't——'

'You did turn me on, Angela.' He ran his fingertip along the line of her jaw, and though she longed to jerk her head away she wasn't prepared to give him that satisfaction. 'And you knew that red would have that effect—no, don't argue.' He shook his head as she opened her mouth to protest. 'So, whatever motives you think you had when you chose red, I'd advise you to look deep inside yourself. You may be surprised at what your subconscious is trying to tell you.'

She shivered as he raised her hand to his lips. His eyes were darkly challenging as he brushed her fingertips with a kiss. 'Your father's watching,' he murmured mockingly. 'Smile, my darling.'

She did smile.

And she kept on smiling.

She smiled through the buffet meal, she smiled through all the speeches—she even smiled, though by this time every little muscle in her face ached with the effort, as she said goodbye to her father and Molly around eight when the party was finally over. She even managed to smile as she kissed Nicky goodnight, in the room which Dominic told him had been his as a child. Exhausted, Nicky was asleep before she and Dominic left the room, Maggie clutched in his arms.

'I'll get him a new stuffed toy next time I'm in town,' Dominic said as he closed the door behind them. 'That threadbare monstrosity should go in the dustbin!'

Angela felt a stab of alarm. 'Don't you dare! Maggie's his favourite toy—he can't get to sleep without her! I mislaid her once, and when I tucked him in that night and there was no Maggie he was in a total panic. I thought I'd never get him calmed down; he just sobbed and sobbed till I eventually found h——'

'Hey, hey, hold on!' Dominic stepped back, his palms held out defensively in front of him. 'Don't worry, I've got the message. I won't touch his precious——'

'Didn't you have a favourite toy when you were a child?' Angela challenged.

'As a matter of fact,' he said with a wry twist of his lips, 'now that you mention it, I did. It was a monkey—his name was . . . Muggles!'

Angela had never imagined Dominic as a child. Now she found herself picturing a miniature version of Dominic the man, cuddled up in bed with a toy monkey, and, despite herself, chuckled.

They had reached the head of the stairs and she felt a twinge of uneasiness as Dominic stopped, blocking her way.

'That is the first time today,' he said softly, 'that I have seen you smile—really smile, I mean. A smile that reached your eyes.'

'What did you expect?' she countered defensively. 'You *ordered* me to smile at the reception and I smiled. More than that I couldn't deliver—if you expected to see a spark of joy as well, I'm sorry. I can't pretend to emotions that I don't feel. Are you worried someone might have guessed——?'

'Oh, no, Angela, my love, there's no question of that—you fooled *everyone* today…except me, of course. You're quite the little actress—but I don't know why that should surprise me! It's not as if it's the first time… How do you do it, Angela? How do you manage to conceal the emotions you're really feeling? It must take a special kind of skill to fool people into thinking you're in love.'

A special kind of skill? If that were true, then it was a skill he himself possessed. Angela compressed her lips as she found herself remembering how convincing he'd been that night by the lake, when he'd told her he loved her. Yet all the time…

'It's not so hard, Dominic.' You should know, she added to herself bitterly, being a past master of the art yourself. 'People believe what they want to believe, they see what they expect to see—wedding guests normally assume they've been invited to the church to watch the marriage of two people who are in love with each other——'

'While we're on the subject——' Dominic's eyes had become hooded, so Angela couldn't read his expression '—what made you change your mind about marrying me? Or was your initial reluctance just a case of playing hard to get?'

Angela hesitated for only a moment before saying in haughty tones, 'Let's just say I changed my mind because it suited my purpose.'

'You're quite a woman.' Dominic's smile was mocking. 'I have to take my hat off to you. It took longer, I'm sure, than you'd planned, but you ended up getting exactly what you wanted.'

'And what, may I ask, was *that*?'

'Me.' He laughed at the look of outraged disbelief on her face. 'That does sound a little arrogant, doesn't it? But when I say "me", I'm not referring to my humble self, but rather to my wealth and position—the wealth and position to which, as my wife, you now have access. They do say, don't they, that the quiet ones are the ones to watch out for? I suppose you started your little campaign years ago, when you wormed your way into my father's affections by pretending to be interested in all the things he was interested in. He was taken in, too, by your apparent sweetness and——'

Angela had never slapped anyone before, never in her life, and she had never expected to. Impulsive though she was, there were certain things, certain actions, that were completely foreign to her nature. But as she listened to Dominic's insulting words, words delivered in a tone of utter contempt, she felt as if something tight inside her had suddenly sprung loose. Her hand swung through the air, almost of its own volition, hitting Dominic's left cheek with a resounding smack. The impact jarred her arm, and stung her palm, but before she could even begin to react to the pain Dominic swung into action.

With a savage oath that made her wince, he grabbed her by the upper arms, anger flaring in his eyes. 'You vicious little animal!' His fingers dug roughly into her flesh. 'My God, you're asking for it, Angela—behave like an animal, and you're going to get treated like one!'

'Let go of me!'

'Not till you listen to what I have to say,' he responded grimly. 'Violence never solved anything——'

'You listen to me!' Panting, she glared up at him defiantly. 'What gives you the right to sit in judgement over me? You know nothing about the relationship I had with your father, and I'm not going to sit back and let you soil it with your nasty——'

'Let's stick to the point, shall we?' His cheek where she had slapped it was deep crimson; the rest of his face was pale. 'Don't ever slap me again,' his voice was harsh and strained, 'because if you do I may forget you're a woman, and hit you right back.'

'What's stopping you now?' she challenged. 'Oh, don't bother to answer that! I know the answer. Dominic the controlled. Always in charge of himself, in charge of any situation in which he finds himself——'

'Believe me, Angela, I've never in my life felt more like hitting anyone—man or woman. But I have certain standards——'

'Oh, I know all about your standards,' she said with a grim little laugh. 'Double standards, that's the kind of standards you have!'

'Now you tell me what *that's* supposed to mean!'

'You want your women to be as pure as the driven snow, while you think it's all right...more than all right!...for you to fool around as much as you like.'

Angela saw his jaw tighten. 'You're wrong about that. There are no *women* in my life—not in the sense you mean—and as for fooling around, as you put it, anyone who does in this day and age is indeed a fool. No, Angela, I don't subscribe to what you call a double standard...not in *any* aspects of my life. I do have standards, though. High standards. And I expect the people I'm closest to, to share those standards. But let's not get into *that*——'

'No, let's not.' Angela's voice was hard. The last thing she'd ever want Dominic to know was how he'd hurt her by seducing her with false promises of love. 'As far as I'm concerned, the past is past. Now, if you don't mind, I'd like to go to my room and——'

'Fine. I asked Nelly earlier to put your case in the Tower Suite.'

'The Tower Suite? I thought *you* were using it. Didn't Patsy put you there when——?'

'Yes, I'm using the Tower Suite.' Dominic's voice was bland. 'We both are.'

'Oh, no, we're not! You've just said you'd respect the conditions I requested before we were married, and now you're saying you want me to sleep with you! I will not——'

'Sleep with me?' Dominic's eyebrows rose in mock astonishment. 'I'm not inviting you to *sleep* with me, my darling wife—there are two beds in the suite.' His tone was one he might have used to explain something to a rather dim-witted child. 'It's out of the question for us to sleep in different rooms, if the servants aren't to suspect that our marriage is the sham that it is.'

'And if I *refuse* to sleep in the same——'

'Ah, but you won't.' His voice was silky. 'Because it's in your interests as much as in mine that everyone believes we're happily married.'

Her interests? His words could only be a shot in the dark—there was no way he could know about her father's precarious health. Still, she felt frustration churning inside her because of course it *was* in her best interests to keep up the charade. If they slept in separate rooms, the servants would start gossiping—there was a chance Nicky might hear something, and repeat it to his grandfather. She just couldn't risk causing him any unnecessary stress.

'All right,' she said in grim tones. 'I don't seem to have any option, do I?'

'I'm afraid not.' He began walking along the hall and she trailed reluctantly after him. 'Now, at least we've got that settled. We can move into the master suite once it's been redecorated—I'll leave that task to you. You'll have *carte blanche*, of course, and——'

'You don't need to show me to the Tower Suite,' she interrupted flatly. 'I know where it is.'

'I'm sure you do, but I'm going to stay upstairs with you. What would everyone think if I were to spend our wedding evening downstairs, while my bride lay alone in the marriage bed, waiting for me?'

'You know as well as I do that everyone's gone home! Patsy and Mike are spending the night at Blackwell Manor, and Starr and Max are on their way to Heathrow——'

'You're forgetting Nelly and the housemaids, my angel,' he reminded her in a gently chiding voice.

They had reached the door of the Tower Suite. When he opened it, he stepped aside, and motioned Angela to go in. She glared at him defiantly for a moment, and then, lips pursed, she passed him. As she did, she brushed against his arm accidentally, and the fleeting touch sent a shudder rippling right through her.

This was going to be worse than she'd thought, she realised with a feeling of panic. How was she going to stand it, being in the same room, sleeping in the same room, with her body reacting so traitorously to his closeness? How was she going to cope with the effect it would have on her... and how was she going to *hide* that effect?

The only thing to do, she told herself, was to keep thinking about Dominic's arrogance, his nastiness, his cruelty. If she could do that, it should be easy to ignore the pheromones which—like tiny invisible witches on tiny invisible broomsticks—were flying back and forth between them constantly, and constantly trying to enthrall her, trying to put her in the mood for love. The mood for romance. So persuasive were they, so successfully were they achieving their purpose, that she could have sworn she heard music...

But she *was* hearing music; it wasn't her imagination. A stereo was playing a Bryan Adams song, and the singer's voice—raw, raspy, and sexy—reached out and drew her like irresistible male fingers, the erotic timbre setting her nerves quivering as if those fingers were caressing her, intimately...

As she moved forward slowly across the marble-tiled foyer, she felt as if she was under some magic spell. The air seemed to throb with yearning, to pulsate with desire, to be rich with the scent of——

Roses.

She came to an abrupt halt inside the sitting-room and, eyes wide, stared at the scene before her. Roses, gorgeous satin-red roses, were everywhere. They were in Waterford crystal vases on the sofa-table, they were in polished silver cups on the buhl desk by the window, they were in white-painted wicker baskets on either side of the green marble hearth. They were in antique urns on the mantelpiece, they were in Caithness glass globes on the coffee-table, they were in tall pewter jugs on the black-lacquered cocktail cabinet...

And beside the cocktail cabinet was a magnificent silver cooler, containing a magnum of Dom Perignon, on ice.

Champagne, a love song, red roses...

A fire crackled a welcome from the hearth, blue velvet curtains were drawn, shutting out the cold October night, muting the sounds of the rising wind.

It was a scene set for seduction.

Her heart thudding against her throat, Angela took in a ragged breath that seemed to turn her lungs inside out, and swung round to face Dominic.

CHAPTER NINE

'RELAX, Angela.'

With a sardonic laugh, Dominic walked past her and abruptly clicked off the stereo. 'All this——' he waved a dismissing arm around the room '—was strictly for the benefit of the servants. Nelly's discreet enough, but the housemaids aren't, so I guarantee that by tomorrow it'll be all over the district of Hadleigh that Mr Elliott of the Hall is utterly besotted with his new wife. Which, of course, was my purpose.'

The rich scent of the roses seemed to Angela to be suddenly, sickeningly cloying. Dominic was playing with her emotions, she realised, as a cat might play with a mouse...and with the same cruel relish. Oh, no doubt he *had* had the servants in mind when he'd arranged this little set-up, but he must have been well aware that she, too, would have been taken in by it, at least momentarily. And that knowledge must have given him some perverse pleasure.

How much longer was she going to let him treat her this way? she asked herself, feeling a hot anger begin to flame inside her...anger that was directed more at herself than at Dominic. Surely, if she had any spunk at all, she would retaliate.

Well, she did have spunk, and lots of it. And she *would* retaliate. But how?

But even as she asked herself the question the answer thrust itself forcefully into her mind; oh, yes, she knew *exactly* how she could pay him back.

Here in his Tower Suite, he had set the scene...and he had given himself the leading role. But she could steal the scene from him; she could take the lead. And she was *going* to take that lead. It was going to be dangerous, though. She would have to be *very* careful . . .

She plucked a perfect scarlet rosebud from a vase on the table by the door, and held it to her nostrils for a moment, making a show of inhaling the sweet fragrance while all the time concentrating on gaining sufficient control over herself to produce a nonchalant smile that would be convincing.

'You fooled me there for a moment, I must admit.' Casually, she gestured with the rosebud. 'But of course I should have realised . . . and believe me, Dominic, romance is the last thing I'm thinking of. I believe I made myself clear on that point when I agreed to this marriage. All I want to do when I go to bed tonight is sleep.'

'If you're tired, please don't stay up on my account. As for myself, I'm going to unwind a bit before I turn in. It's been a hectic day——'

'Like you,' she said smoothly, 'I'm far too wound up to think of going to bed. I think I'll have a bath and then change into something comfortable and relax for a while too. Oh . . . hadn't you better open the champagne? Nelly would be suspicious tomorrow if she found the bottle unopened.'

Not waiting for his response, she sailed with an appearance of confidence past him through an open doorway, which she prayed would lead to the bedroom and not into a bathroom or her exit would be ruined.

It *was* the bedroom, thank heavens . . . and a splendid bedroom at that, with its vast space and rounded walls. At the far end were the two beds Dominic had mentioned earlier, massive king-sized beds with impressive blue and silver silk canopies. The floor-length curtains were of the same blue and silver fabric, the round walls were lined with pale blue damask worsted, and the floor was covered with a carpet so sumptuously thick that when she kicked off her high-heeled pumps the silver plush almost tickled her ankles.

Tossing the scarlet rosebud on to the dressing-table, she walked across to the smaller of the two mahogany wardrobes, and tugged open the door. As she'd hoped, she found, hanging inside, the clothes she'd packed in her case the previous evening.

She could feel her pulse racing as she reached for the padded hanger on which was draped her wedding present from Molly, a black pure silk nightdress whose matching négligé was trimmed with Austrian lace and midnight pearls. 'Men love black,' the older woman had whispered confidently when she'd come over with the gift the night before. 'And you have a gorgeous figure.' Her eyes had twinkled. 'Give that man of yours a wedding night to remember.'

Yes, Angela had reflected tautly, she would give Dominic a wedding night to remember, if for no other reason than that she wasn't going to sleep with him! Nevertheless, she had taken the gift with her, afraid to leave it at the cottage in case Molly or her father chanced to find it... but she had also packed the cotton pyjamas which she usually wore, and which she'd meant to put on tonight. But of course she hadn't dreamed that she'd be planning to seduce Dominic... or at least lead him on till he was at the point of no return... before rejecting him!

Adrenalin pumped through her veins as she made for the bathroom, and it speeded up for a heart-lurching moment as she heard the unmistakable sound of the champagne cork popping through in the sitting-room. She really didn't have a head for liquor. At social functions she always limited herself to one glass of alcohol—any more and she became quite giddy and foolish. She would have to watch herself, just sip at her drink...

Locking the bathroom door behind her, she draped the nightdress and négligé over the blue and silver cushioned chair by the bath, and, leaning over the white, claw-footed bathtub, turned on the taps.

*   *   *

'I think I'd like a glass of that champagne now.' The smile Angela had been practising in the bathroom trembled on her lips as she addressed Dominic.

He hadn't heard her come through from the bedroom, and she'd stood in the doorway for a long moment before she spoke, her intentions weakening, traitorously, as she'd looked at him. He was sitting on the sofa in front of the fire . . . but though he was lying back with his eyes shut, one leg crossed over the other at the knee, the relaxed lines of his body were belied by the tautly drawn lines of his face. She felt an involuntary urge to go over and kneel down at his side, gently smooth back the swath of black hair that had tumbled over his furrowed brow, run a fingertip down the grooves that were grimly etched on either side of his mouth. He looked exhausted, she realised, utterly stressed out, as if he desperately needed some tender loving care . . .

Straightening her shoulders determinedly, she compressed her lips. What *he* badly needed was to get some of his own medicine—and she was the one who was going to administer it. And if everything went as she planned he was going to find that medicine rather unpleasant.

Now, as he heard her say she was ready for some champagne, he stirred.

Opening his eyes, he got to his feet and, without looking at her, made for the silver cooler. 'I didn't think you'd take so long,' he said. 'I hope all the bubbles haven't gone out of the bubbly.'

As he poured the champagne into two fluted crystal glasses, Angela crossed to the stereo. To set the mood, to set the trap, she needed all the help she could get. As she switched on the music again, Bryan Adams's voice rasped into the air like a caress of purple-frosted velvet. To her dismay, the sensual, rough-smooth sound vibrated right through her, quivering all the way to her soul.

This was dangerous, far too dangerous. It was Dominic's self-control she wanted to weaken, not her own!

Running the tip of her tongue over her lips, she made to switch the sound off, but as she reached out she caught a glimpse of her reflection in a mirror on the wall above the stereo and froze.

The mirror in the bathroom had been steamed after her bath, and, though she had swiped at it with a towel, her reflection had still been misty. In this mirror, it was clear and sharp. She had never thought of herself as sexy-looking, but tonight, in black silk, she barely recognised the sultry siren facing her... and as she stared at her reflection, and ran a bewildered hand through her lustrous blonde hair, she realised that the impact was caused by the stark contrast between the innocence in her frank grey eyes, and the seductive promise of the black silk nightdress as it clung to her feminine curves with tantalising allure.

The garment was cut so low that, had it not been for the ruched edging of black lace, her nipples would have been revealed. Her first impulse when she saw how exposed she was, was to pull the négligé across to conceal her near nakedness, but when she tried she found it wasn't possible; the filmy pearled garment was designed to act only as a showcase for her breasts—the way a picture frame might set off the picture inside it.

What was she going to——?

Dominic's reflection appeared behind her in the mirror, two glasses in his hands. In the fleeting glimpse she got of him before she lowered her eyes to hide her panic, she saw him pause abruptly, saw his eyes narrow to green slits. She also saw the banks of roses surrounding him, filling every corner of the room, and the sight brought with it a memory of his contemptuous, 'Relax, Angela... all this was strictly for the benefit of the servants.' And as the words echoed in her brain she felt her vow to pay him back renew itself with an intensity that forcefully strengthened her weakening resolve.

'Thanks, Dominic.' She took the glass, brushing his thumb with the tips of her fingers as she did, and acting as if she hadn't noticed the brief moment of touching. With an effort she ignored the little tingling sensation that had run up her arm. Forcing her lips into a smile, she walked across the room and sat down in the left-hand corner of the sofa, on the cushion he'd just vacated. The seat was still warm. She found that disturbing, but she ignored that too.

'Oh...' she glanced up at him, her eyebrows raised in guileless question '...you were sitting here. Should I move?'

He was still standing over by the stereo. He was still staring at her. She was quite unable to read the expression on his face, but when he spoke his voice had a strangled quality. 'Sit where you are.'

'Thanks.' She gave him a cool smile.

He cleared his throat. 'In the circumstances...' his voice was steadier now but Angela noticed his fingers tightening around the stem of his glass '...do you think that's appropriate?'

'What do you mean, Dominic?' Angela was pleased with the faint edge of puzzlement she gave to her tone.

His Adam's apple twitched slightly. 'That...black thing.'

'Oh, *this*!' Allowing an amused smile to play around her lips, Angela fingered the lace edging of the night-dress, the edging that barely covered her nipples. 'Relax...it's strictly for the benefit of the servants.' She kept all traces of sarcasm from her tone as she parroted his earlier words. 'You're right in thinking it's important we present the appropriate kind of picture to the servants. I agree with you one hundred per cent. After all, what if Nelly or one of the housemaids were to bring me a cup of tea tomorrow morning and found me in my cotton jammies?'

Chuckling, Angela curled her left leg under her, and then, with a great play of gathering her nightdress around her as if she were making sure she was decently covered, she let it fall so that her other leg was naked from mid-thigh down. With an absent smile, she leaned into the corner, and began swinging her right leg idly above the carpet, tapping the fingers of her left hand on the padded arm of the sofa in time to the music.

She saw his gaze flicker over her thigh, over her knees, over her calf, down to her ankle, and down even further, where it lingered. And as it did she suddenly remembered something he'd said to her, that night by the lake...

'Angela, my love, you have the sexiest feet in the world.'

She had answered in a whisper, 'Feet aren't sexy, Dominic.'

At that, he had placed one of her hands over his heart, and asked huskily, 'Then how would you explain this?' *This* had been the hammering of his heart, which sounded to her as if it had gone berserk.

Now, five years later, he seemed transfixed once more by her feet, and she felt her heartbeats give a quick patter of excitement. Seducing him was going to be easier than she thought.

'This couch,' she said casually, 'is quite comfortable. Perhaps one of us could sleep through here. That would give us both more privacy.'

'Not a good idea.' The fire crackled and hissed, sending sparks sputtering up the chimney. 'Nicky might come in before we're awake——'

'Couldn't we lock the door?'

'And have Nelly and the housemaids wonder just what's going on in the Tower Suite at night?' Dominic raised his eyebrows ironically. 'No, my dear little wife—definitely not! Besides, sleeping on a sofa may be bearable for a couple of nights, but over the long term it's just not feasible.'

Angela lifted her shoulders in a couldn't-care-less kind of shrug. 'It was just a thought.'

If only, she thought uneasily as she stared into the fire, Dominic weren't so damnably sexually attractive. It was almost as if a trail of gunpowder ran between them, and every time they were together the connection sparked a flame that ignited the gunpowder, which sizzled its way to her and engulfed her in a raging fire.

It was happening now. She felt as if her flesh was burning, as if her whole body was being consumed. And he wasn't even touching her.

She held her breath tensely as he crossed the room. Would he sit beside here? No, he didn't. As she watched, he lowered himself into an armchair by the fire—the one furthest from where she herself was sitting—and she uttered a silent prayer of thanks. He would only have to brush against her, she knew, and she would melt into his arms. Yet she knew also that if her plan was going to work they would have to touch...

More than touch.

But it would be on her terms. And at a moment of her choosing. A moment when she felt totally in control of herself, and those treacherous pheromones. And right now, she knew, was *not* the moment!

'How's your drink?' he asked.

'Oh...' She'd forgotten about it. Sipping from the glass, she felt bubbles tickling her nose, felt the liquid dance like moonbeams down her throat. 'It's delicious,' she murmured, already feeling it singing in her blood. She would, of course, have only this one glass...which would be just the perfect amount to supply her with Dutch courage. Sipping slowly, she found she was actually enjoying it very much, and, tipping the glass, savoured it to the last drop.

As she did, Dominic asked, 'Would you like some more?'

About to say, No, thanks, she hesitated. The thought had flitted into her mind that Dominic would certainly suspect something was up if she suddenly changed from being cool and distant to being amenable to his advances. Unless, of course he believed her to be tipsy.

'Mmm, all right.' She threw him a smile. 'It's very moreish.' With a graceful arching of her arm, she held up her glass, and as she did she thought she saw a flicker of desire in his eyes, but when she saw the mocking glitter a moment later she decided she must have been mistaken.

'Moreish? What the devil does *that* mean—is it a new yuppie word?'

'Heavens, no, it's been around for ages! It just refers to something that's so pleasant you want more. Usually something to eat or drink. Haven't you heard the expression before?'

'No,' he said over his shoulder as he walked across to the champagne cooler. 'I haven't.' He refilled her glass and recrossed the room. 'But if anything in this world is "moreish", it is Dom Perignon!'

He lifted his own glass from the coffee-table, and went back to refill it. As he did, Angela twisted round on her cushion, and, reaching across the back of the sofa, upturned her glass and poured the champagne into a crystal vase on the sofa-table behind her.

By the time Dominic had turned back, she was sitting casually in the corner again, holding her glass to her lips and pretending to sip from it, while spreading her fingers around the fluted contours in such a way that the contents—or rather the lack of them—were hidden from view.

He sat down in the armchair again, and put his drink on the hammered brass table at his side. He looked much more relaxed than he had a few minutes before, Angela reflected—perhaps the champagne was beginning to loosen him up.

She, herself, was much less tense, now that she felt herself in control of the situation. Half closing her eyes, she stared into the fire, and in a few moments began to feel almost lulled to sleep by the radiant warmth from the red-hot coals, the rough-velvet voice of Bryan Adams, the romantic scent of the roses——

It was the champagne, she realised with a start, that had put her in this dangerously relaxed mood. Was it more potent than the wine she was used to? Straightening, she glanced at Dominic from under her lashes, and found him watching her. She moved her lips so that they formed a smile. Then, pretending once again to drink from her glass, she tilted it as if pouring the last of the champagne down her throat.

Affecting a contented sigh, she leaned forward and placed the empty glass on the table, letting it topple, and then catching it with a startled, 'Oops—almost broke it,' before setting it straight with exaggerated care.

'It is a distinctly moreish champagne.' Dominic's voice held a hint of amusement. 'And since, after all, this is our wedding night and—as you mentioned—Nelly will be examining the bottle tomorrow, perhaps we should have another glass.'

Angela formed her mouth into a rueful smile as he got to his feet. 'I really don't have a head for liquor, Dominic——'

'In that case——'

'But if you insist perhaps I'll have just one more. Make it a teensy one.'

He really was devilishly attractive. Angela shook her head as she watched him cross the room. He had such gorgeous black hair, such wonderful shoulders, such a sexy way of walking. Too bad he was such a rat——

'Your drink, *madame*.'

The rat was standing in front of her, a smile slanting his face. He held out her glass—which was full—and as Angela took it from him she pretended to have a little difficulty focusing on it. Their fingers brushed lightly, and she almost winced as she felt a tingling sensation run through her body.

This time, he had refilled his own glass at the same time as he'd refilled hers, depriving her of the oppor-

tunity to pour her own champagne into the vase. But as
Angela tried to figure out how to get rid of her drink
without his noticing he set his glass down on the table
and, crouching by the fire, started pushing the hot coals
around with the brass poker. But just as she began to
twist round so that she could dispose of her drink in the
same way as she had the previous one he straightened
abruptly and turned to face her. Heart hammering,
Angela froze where she sat, her body half twisted.

'It's damned warm in here.' Amazingly, he seemed to
see nothing strange about her grotesquely contorted position. Tugging his tie open, he loosened the top button
of his shirt. 'I think I'll take a leaf out of your book
and change into something more comfortable.'
Scratching a hand through his hair, he made for the
bedroom with a careless, 'Be right back.'

Angela's breath hissed out as he disappeared into the
other room. Leaning forward, she poured her drink into
one of the glass globes on the coffee-table. There—she
heaved a sigh of relief as she slumped back in her seat—
that got rid of that! Now, when Dominic came back,
she would put her plan into action.

She didn't hear him return. He was gone for such a
long time that she had drifted off into a world of her
own. Staring into the fire, she watched pictures form in
the flames, and she was lost in a bewitching scene of
scarlet-sheeted yachts and purple seas when he walked
in front of her, blocking out her view. Involuntarily, she
looked up... and felt her heart stagger as her gaze en-
compassed him. He was barefooted, and had changed
into a black robe that was belted and came barely to his
knees. Black hair curled over his legs, curled over his
muscled forearms, curled at the V-neck of the robe. He
looked, she thought giddily, like every woman's dream
of what a man should be. Trying not to hyperventilate,
she raised her eyes to his face.

And felt a great lurch of panic. What a mistake she
had made! How could she ever have thought she was

capable of leading this man on and then spurning him? Even now, though he wasn't even touching her, she felt herself responding dizzily to his closeness, felt her flesh answering the call of his, aching for his caress. Like a wild horse straining to be free, her body trembled, and she felt consumed by an uncontrollable hunger. Oh, thank heavens it wasn't too late to change her mind...for change her mind she must. She was absolutely no match for this man. And her only hope of salvation, she knew, was to avoid his touch...for once she was in his arms she would be lost.

'Stand up,' he said in a terse tone, holding out his right hand.

She stared at it. But in her foggy, distraught state what she saw was not a hand, but an apple...and Adam, the roles reversed, holding out the tempting fruit to Eve. She shook her head, not meeting his eyes. 'What...what do you want?' She twined her own hands together in her lap and her gaze fixed on her ruby ring, glittering, unfamiliar——

She heard an impatient exclamation, and then, even as she gasped in protest, he was grasping her twined fingers, and, despite her trying to fight him, he had tugged her to her feet. She stumbled a little, trying to regain her balance, but before she could he had put his arms around her and pulled her against him, crushing her breasts against his chest. She was trapped, in a matter of seconds, in his powerful, inescapable embrace.

She managed a gasping, 'What are you doing? Let me go; I don't want——'

'Don't *want*?' he interrupted her, his green eyes taunting. 'Don't tell me, darling wife, that you don't *want*! Your body language, your clothing, your voice— they've all been telling me since we came into this room that you do, indeed, *want*. And what you want, on your wedding night, you should get.' He smiled, a cruel, hard smile. 'Don't you agree?'

When he'd circled her with his arms, he'd trapped her hands between their bodies; now she felt them digging into his ribs. She tried to release them, but no matter how she strained she couldn't move them an inch. 'Let me go,' she panted. 'I want to go to bed.'

'Good—that's what I want too.' He was still imprisoning her, but with only one arm now; she could feel the other hand cup her head, feel him drawing her closer, so that their faces were almost touching—their lips were almost touching. And Angela felt dismay clutch at her heart as she became suddenly aware of the fragrance from his skin...from his jaw...

Aftershave lotion.

He had shaved; that was why he had taken so long. And a man shaved before going to bed only when he expected to——

'That's not what I meant,' she whispered, fighting down her panic.

'But that was part of your game, wasn't it?'

'Game?' She was suddenly finding it difficult to breathe. 'What...game?'

'To get me into bed. And then to pretend...after we'd made love...that you were so tipsy you hadn't known what you were doing. The perfect cop-out. Oh, it was a cunning little plan, I grant you that...and I realise you came up with it because you were desperate to satisfy that voracious sexual appetite of yours at any cost——'

'Pretend...to be tipsy?' How on earth had he guessed? It was as if he could read her mind. 'How did I know?' he asked. 'I saw you in the mirror, my darling deceiver, pouring your second glass of champagne into a vase...and I imagine you disposed of your third glass in the same way...'

Oh, dear God—no wonder he'd looked so relaxed when he'd sat back in his chair earlier. She'd knocked him off balance by appearing in the black nightdress, but when he'd spotted her pouring out her champagne he'd once more felt himself in control of the situation. And Dominic Elliott, she knew only too well, liked always to be in control.

'All right...' she tried to keep her voice steady '...so you saw me pour out my drink. But you totally misread my intentions. I didn't mean to go to bed with you. I meant only to——' She broke off, feeling herself floundering. The last thing she wanted was for him to know what her plan was.

'Ah, so you didn't plan to go as far as the bedroom.' In his slowly spoken words, she could hear the dawning realisation of the truth. 'You did mean to lead me on, though, to tantalise me, till I was yours for the taking. And then...what? Break off at the last moment? Leave me in an agony of frustration?' As he muttered the words, fiercely, he yanked her even closer against himself, and now she could feel every line, every angle of his body against her own, even through his bulky robe, and she felt her heart give a series of erratic, lurching beats as she was made painfully aware that he was already aroused to a point of extreme frustration. 'A dangerous game, Angela,' he murmured. 'But...since you've already embarked on it, I'm going to insist you carry it out to the bitter end.'

'No! You can't! I——'

'Sorry.' His wavy hair had tumbled over his brow, and his jaw was set grimly, giving him a savage expression. 'When you tease a tiger, my little temptress, you can't expect it to become suddenly tame when you decide the game is over. You've teased me, and you must know by now that you've already achieved exactly the results you wanted. Doesn't that make you pleased with yourself? To know that all you have to do is flaunt yourself in a black nightie and you have me foaming at the mouth? So...this is your cue. Wasn't it at this point that you were planning to tell me that...you've suddenly developed a *headache*?'

It had been an exhausting day. Now, as Dominic leered down at her, all at once Angela could take it no more.

'Yes!' she said, with a forceful wrench that freed herself from his arms. 'I do have a headache. It seems that every time I'm around you I get one. I don't know why, but you just have that effect on me.' To her horror, she felt tears welling in her eyes, heard her voice break, but she went on because she couldn't stop now; it was as if a spring had burst forth from the ground and the words were gushing out like water. 'So it's just as well, isn't it, that this isn't going to be a real marriage, because even if I did want to make love with you I wouldn't be able to enjoy it because of my constant headaches?' Hardly knowing what she was doing, she rubbed away the tears that were tumbling down her cheeks, tears that seemed to be gushing out as uncontrollably as her words, and then she pressed her hands against her temples. 'But I don't want to make love with you, Dominic, I don't, I don't, I don't—I only wanted to pay you back for being so cruel, for setting the scene you did here, with the music, the champagne, the red roses, making me think you really wanted to——'

She broke off with a cry as he grasped her wrists and, in the space of a heartbeat, had her hands pinned behind her back, her body trapped against his again. Helpless, she dug her teeth into her lower lip and stared up at him mutely.

'This is what I really want,' he rasped, desire clouding the clear emerald of his eyes so that the pupils looked like misted green glass. 'I want you. God, how I want you... and since you're my wife, and I know that despite your lies and protests you want me too...'

His lips crushed fiercely on hers, and his grip on her wrists snapped tighter as he jerked them mercilessly against the small of her back. She felt a very real fear taking seed inside her. Surely... surely this man wasn't going to take her against her will? Wasn't going to...*rape* her? She might have been mistaken about him in some .

ways, she acknowledged as she struggled, panting, in a futile attempt to free herself, but it was unthinkable that, no matter how he might have changed, the Dominic she had once known could even consider such a thing. Yet——

She could feel his arms, the muscles hard and corded, like prison bars confining her body; she could feel his fingers, strong and cold as steel claws, restraining her wrists; she could feel his thighs, aggressive, powerful, compelling, thrusting against the curve of her hip; she could feel his manhood—her mouth was suddenly dry as desert sand—pulsing with hot urgency against the plane of her belly...

And lower.

Oh, God... She moaned deep in her throat, in anguished protest, as liquid desire began to trickle through her. It came slowly at first, trembling and hesitant, as if unsure what to do, where to go. But then, as she felt the persistent thrust of a knee prising her thighs apart, the trickle quickly became a stream, and within moments that stream had become a wild and burning river, flooding through her body, to every cell, to every tingling nerve-ending, surging and rushing and spreading, tantalising and seducing, till she was no longer flesh and blood, but a writhing, yielding, sensual——

Her teeth had been dug deeply into her lower lip before he started his assault; now, to her dismay, she realised her lips were parted, and his tongue was tangling, coiling with her own. When had she accepted his invitation to join with him in this erotic, intimate mating dance? she asked herself in horror. When had she lost all control of her sane and sensible side, and let her voluptuous side, her wanton side take over? But even as she asked herself the unanswerable question she heard Dominic groan. It was a sound that seemed to come from his heart, from his soul, from the very depths of his being. And it was a sound that demolished the last vestiges of her sane and sensible self, and left her a slave to the other—a slave to the wild, passionate Angela who had been straining inside her from the moment she'd seen Dominic again. She'd tried to fight herself at first ... but now all she could do was give in. She had neither the will, nor the strength to resist.

Catching Dominic unexpectedly, she tore her wrists from his slackened grip, and, winding her arms with a choking cry around his neck, she arched her slender body against him in woman's ancient indication of consent and surrender, feeling a rush of euphoria and a thrill of excitement and anticipation as she felt her soft and most sensitive flesh brush erotically against the hard ridge of his arousal.

For just a second she felt Dominic freeze. Then she heard him moan, felt him wrap his arms around her in a cradling embrace that melded together every curve and every plane of their bodies, fitting them together as perfectly as two pieces of a jigsaw. In some distant floating part of her mind, Angela realised that, given a choice, she would never move again. This was where she wanted to be, forever more, in Dominic's arms...

He was the first to move. With a thickly murmured, 'Oh, Angela, my love...' he dragged his lips over her cheek, planting little kisses wherever he went. Then on he went to trace the delicate curve of her jaw, the pure line of her throat. She closed her eyes as the smooth, clean-shaven plane of his jaw slid down over her neck, she threw her head back in ecstasy as he began foraging in the scented hollows of her collarbone. He planted increasingly hungry kisses wherever he trespassed, his hands moving urgently over her silk-clad back, his lips caressing her skin in a way that caused the blood to course in an exquisite rush to her nipples. Nipples that had peaked to hard nubs at his very first touch.

The game-playing was over. Angela knew that Dominic was now no longer in control of his actions; he was being blindly led by the inexorable passion that had them both in its spell. Like slaves under a ruthless master, their wills were bent to its demands. He stroked and she moaned, he asked and she gave, he led and she followed . . .

And when she found herself being picked up like a fragile toy in his muscular arms the little mew that came from her lips was not a mew of protest, but a mew of wanting, a mew of frustration that his body was no longer pressed close to hers. And all the while, as he carried her through to the bedroom, her arms were locked tightly around his neck, and, all the time, their kiss was uninterrupted. Even when he unfastened his black robe and he shrugged it from his wide shoulders he didn't release her lips; even when he gently removed her arms from around his neck and slid off her négligé and the silken black web of lace that lay underneath he didn't release her lips. Only when she was finally lying on the bed, the silk bedspread like cool water under her heated flesh, his naked body covering hers, his weight supported by his hands on either side of her head, did he finally draw his lips from hers.

Their eyes met, and Angela felt a swooning sensation in her head as she looked up into the glazed green depths of his gaze. His face was pale except for a flush on his cheekbones; his forehead and his upper lip gleamed with perspiration; his thick black hair was wildly tangled. As if it was the most natural thing in the world, Angela raised one hand and ran it through the glossy strands. She saw his eyelids flicker.

'You're mine now, Angela.' His voice was husky, his breath hot and intimate on her cheeks, on her lips. 'Mine alone, now and forever more.'

Angela closed her eyes as another surging wave of desire swept through her, desire so intense that this time it made her feel faint. She was aware of Dominic's lips moving in her hair, aware that he was whispering sweet carnal words in her ear. The words stimulated a swollen heat between her thighs, a quivering, seeking heat, and, as his palms slid over her thrusting nipples again and again and again, his lips found hers once more and he kissed her moist, trembling mouth with a tenderness and a hunger that stole her soul.

No man could kiss a woman in such a way unless he was in love with her . . .

It was Angela's last rational thought. A moment later she was adrift on a sea of ecstasy, as Dominic, with his lips, his hands, and his body, took her to a place where worldly things were forgotten and the pleasures of the flesh reigned supreme.

CHAPTER TEN

WHEN Angela woke next morning, she expected to find Dominic lying beside her in the bed, but on stretching out a questing hand under the covers all she found was the cool surface of the sheet where he had been earlier.

Hearing the curtains being drawn, she stretched lazily before pushing herself up on her elbow. 'Dominic?' she murmured, blinking in the dazzle of sunlight.

But it wasn't Dominic; it was Nelly. The elderly housekeeper, her ample figure restrained by her starched blue uniform, was crossing the room, a small tray in her hands. Fumbling with the bedcovers, Angela quickly pulled up the top sheet to cover herself.

'It's only me, ma'am. Mr Elliott asked me to bring you up a cup of coffee.' The grey-haired woman placed the tray on the bedside table. 'Will there be anything else, Mrs Elliott?' she asked.

'Where's Nicky? Is he up, Nelly?'

'Yes, ma'am. He's with his father—they've gone down to the stables.'

Angela smiled. 'Thanks, Nelly.'

As the housekeeper left the room Angela pushed back the covers and slid her legs off the edge of the bed. At her feet, she noticed as she glanced down, were her black nightie and négligé...and Dominic's black robe.

She scooped them up, and tossed them on the bed. And then, impulsively, she reached for his robe again. Hugging it to her, she buried her face in it and inhaled the familiar musky scent. The erotic memories provoked by the tantalising fragrance made her ache to have his arms around her, made her ache to have his lips on hers.

Pushing herself off the bed, she stood up, and, slipping on the robe, she belted the roomy garment around herself. It came almost to her ankles. With her hands stuffed into the deep pockets, she crossed to the window and looked out.

It was a beautiful day, sunny and dry, and the park was a glorious palette of autumn golds, scarlets and rusts. Angela stretched luxuriously, relishing the wonderful feeling of well-being Dominic's lovemaking had created.

Dreamily, she leaned back against the wall, her eyes drifting over the scene below. Beyond the yew hedge, and the pool, was the trail leading to the stables. In her mind's eye she saw Dominic there, with the horses, his muscles rippling under his shirt as he worked with them ...

She pushed herself from the wall. Why was she lingering up here in the house? Why wasn't she with him? She looked at the pot of coffee, steaming on the tray, and a little smile curved her lips. What she wanted, what she needed, at this moment, wasn't coffee!

Crossing the room with quick steps, she threw open her wardrobe and drew out a navy sweatshirt, a pair of jeans, and clean undies. Then, humming under her breath, she walked into the bathroom, and turned on the taps for her shower.

'Excuse me, I'm looking for Mr Elliott.' Angela stuffed her hands into the pockets of her sweatshirt as she addressed the tow-haired youth who was leading a glossy brown stallion from the stables in the direction of the oval track. 'Have you any idea where I might find him?'

'In there, ma'am.' The lad jerked a thumb towards the stables. 'He's showing his boy Suki's kittens. They're seven weeks old today.' He continued on his way, the sound of his booted feet on the cobbled yard mingling with the clip-clop of the stallion's hoofs.

Angela took in a deep breath, savouring the earthy smell of the countryside, and, as she wandered through the large open doorway of the cavernous whitewashed building that comprised the stables, the smell of hay, leather, and horses.

On either side of her as she stepped along past the stalls horses looked out at her, their liquid eyes bright and alert. Her trainers made little sound and as she approached the far end of the building she heard Nicky's voice. It came from an empty stall to her right, and she found herself smiling as she crept up to the open door.

'This is the one I like best, Daddy. May I have it?'

Angela leaned against the door-jamb, a feeling of warmth and joy in her heart as she saw the two together. They were utterly oblivious of her. Nicky was sitting on a pile of hay, with a fluffy grey and white kitten cradled in his arm, and behind him, in a hollow, was nestled a huge tabby with several more kittens swarming over her. Dominic, wearing jeans, a rough denim shirt and leather boots, was crouched down beside him.

'Son, they're *all* yours, if you want them.' He grinned. 'You won't be able to bring them into the house, though. One of Nelly's rules—no animals indoors. But you can come down here and play with them any time, so long as you ask your mother or me first.'

Angela felt her pulse-rate quicken as she let her eyes roam over Dominic's wide shoulders, loving the way the denim fabric stretched over the hard muscles, loving the way his thick black hair tapered at his nape, loving the clever, tanned fingers that were now stroking the kitten. And as she watched she felt a sudden fullness in her breasts, remembering how those same clever fingers had caressed her nipples last night—and a sudden quiver of desire as she remembered how those same clever fingers had later subjected her to such exquisite torment...

She cleared her throat, and Dominic straightened quickly at the sound and turned round. Their eyes met, and she felt her cheeks turn warm. There was no way he could avoid seeing the heavy look of desire in hers, no way he could avoid seeing the eager thrust of her breasts, stimulated by the memory of what had happened between them.

'Good morning, Dominic.' Her voice was husky, sensual.

'Mummy! Mummy!' Nicky tumbled across the hay towards her and stood between them, the kitten in his arms. 'Look at the kitty—isn't she neat? I'm going to call her Fluff!'

'She's darling!' As Angela spoke, even though she had bent to hug her son, she wasn't looking at him; she was looking at Dominic. But what she saw in his face brought a shiver of foreboding to her heart. His green eyes—eyes which had been laughing with Nicky a moment before— were now shuttered. His whole expression was shuttered.

Once again, he was closing her out.

She felt herself shrink back as if he had hit her.

'Dominic...?' She straightened, her hands on Nicky's shoulders for support as she felt her legs grow weak. 'What's...?'

'Good morning, Angela.' Dominic's lips moved in an impersonal smile—the kind of smile he might have given a passing stranger. 'Come down to see the kittens, have you?'

The wall he had put up between them was so effective that she could almost see it—thick, brick, and impenetrable.

'Nicky,' he went on, 'would you stay here, for a minute or two? I want to talk with your mother.'

'All right, Daddy.' With the kitten clawing her way up over his shoulder, the child clambered back over the hay, and sprawled down comfortably. Picking up a piece of hay, he pulled the kitten from his shirt, and began teasing her.

Feeling as if she was on her way to the guillotine, Angela walked back, past the stalls, past the horses, to the stable door, and she stopped right outside it. She had heard Dominic's steps just behind her, all the way, firm, relentless, determined. A man with a purpose.

'Over here.' His command was tersely uttered, and, grasping her by the elbow, he ushered her away from the stables and across the road to the edge of the nearest paddock. There, he released her, and, turning away abruptly, leaned against the wooden fence, his elbows resting on the top rail. On the grassy stretch beyond, three colts were frolicking, their haunches glistening in the sunshine. Beyond, on the oval track, the tow-headed youth was putting the brown stallion through its paces.

'Last night,' Dominic said in a harsh voice, 'was a mistake.' He turned with a sudden, jerky movement, and faced her again, thrusting his hands into the pockets of his jeans as he did. 'A big mistake... and my mistake. But it won't happen again; that I promise you. You have my word... and my apology.'

No, this couldn't be happening; he couldn't be doing this to her, not after... not after the tenderness of his lovemaking, not after the intimacy they had shared. Angela felt all the colour draining from her face. 'You don't have to apologise,' she said in a shaking voice. 'I know we had an agreement, but... I... was the one who made the terms.' She swallowed, hard. It was difficult for her to talk about her feelings, it always had been, but she wasn't going to let him slip away from her, not if she could do something to stop him. 'We... we can change the terms.' With an anguished grimace, she stepped towards him. 'I can't go back, Dominic... back to the way we've been, fighting, saying awful things to each other. We've got something so good, something so very special between us—something most people never experience their whole lives. How can you say it was a mistake?' Her whispered plea was spoken through the tears aching in her throat. 'It was wonderful——'

'Pheromones.' His wide shoulders lifted in a shrug, his lips curved in a taunting smile. 'Pheromones, my dear Angela... you of all people know how potent they can be... how they can beguile us into doing things we shouldn't. Oh, we had good sex, I'm not denying that—

great sex, if you will! But I've had great sex before, and I know you have too. Variety is the spice of life, right?'

He was the only man she'd ever slept with—why did he seem convinced she was promiscuous? What had happened in his life to make him so cruel and so cynical? She cradled her arms around herself as if she could in that way assuage the pain slicing through her heart. In some vague part of her mind she wondered if blood was seeping through her sweatshirt—if the wound was as deep as it felt, there should certainly be blood... '*Good sex,*' she echoed in a pleading voice. 'Is that all it was to you?'

'That's all. I assume by the pallor of your face, and your whining tone, that you want more. My God, is there no *end* to what you want? Let me see...' Ticking the items off with his fingers, he made no effort to conceal his anger as he went on, contemptuously, 'First, you wanted me to publicly agree I was the father of your child, secondly you wanted everything your own way on our wedding-day, thirdly, and despite our agreement that there would be no physical contact when we were alone, you wanted sex on your wedding night...' He threw out his hands in a gesture of mock despair. 'You got everything you wanted—and now you want more—you want a happy-ever-after ending too?' He stepped so close to her that she could almost feel his rage like a slap. 'Sorry, Angela, love, no way. Oh, you can have good sex every night of the week, if you wish...but if you want a doting husband too you've married the wrong man.'

She stared up into his eyes, hardly able to believe what she was hearing. He was willing to have sex with her...but that was all.

'Dominic.' With every bit of strength she had in her, she kept her pain from showing in her voice. 'I think there's something I should make clear to you so you won't continue to labour under any misapprehensions. I married you—not to have sex, good or otherwise—but because I found out my father has a serious heart problem. He doesn't know that I know—but marrying you was my only way out of a situation that was causing him a great deal of stress.' In clipped tones, she briefly outlined the ramifications of that situation. 'Don't talk, just listen!' she snapped as he opened his mouth to say something. 'If it weren't for that, I'd take Nicky and leave the Hall right now, and be glad to be out of your life forever. As it is, I'm trapped. You talk about all the things I wanted...well, I want one thing more. I want never to have to sleep in the same room as you again. I don't care how you arrange it, I don't care what you say to the servants—the only person I care about is my father, and I'll make sure, somehow, that he never finds out that our marriage is a travesty.'

She whirled on her heel and walked away from him. She had felt, a few minutes ago, as if she was on her way to the guillotine. Of course, she hadn't been—the very idea was laughable. Dominic hadn't cut off her head, he hadn't killed her...

But he had killed something. He had killed the tender emotions he'd drawn so skilfully from her the night before. Those emotions, those wonderful, aching emotions, were now dead. What she had felt for him was now dead. She didn't care, any more, about Dominic Elliott.

And she would never, as long as she lived, let herself care about him again.

That afternoon, Dominic called her back as she was leaving the lunch table and told her, without meeting her eyes, that he was going to be out of the country for several days—the gelding he'd wanted to buy on the day of the christening was once more available and he was going across to the States to try to buy it, and then visit friends.

He had, she realised, found a perfect—if temporary—way to make sure the servants didn't find out they weren't sleeping together.

He left that evening, and, once gone, stayed away. She alone knew that his daily phone calls home were just

to keep Nelly and the servants from becoming suspicious; he spent most of the time talking to Nicky.

The days passed slowly by, and the weather grew more
dismal. The skies were mournful, and in the afternoons
the sun would sink in a blood-red glow behind the woods.
Angela's own depressed state blended in so well with the
dull weather that she found herself spending much of
her time outdoors. She hadn't been eating well, she
couldn't sleep—she couldn't settle to do anything but
tramp around the estate, her mind in a despairing
turmoil.

On the eighth day after Dominic's departure, it rained
all morning. Right after lunch, it stopped, and Angela
took Nicky for a walk, though they didn't stay out long.
They were on their way back to the house, Nicky
chortling as he squelched through piles of soggy autumn
leaves in his black wellingtons, when they saw a mid-
night-blue Volvo come wheeling at a steady pace round
the curve of the drive.

'Who can that be?' Angela murmured.

'It's Aunt Patsy!' Nicky said in an astonished voice
as the car drove by and the driver waved a gay greeting.

'So it is!' Although Mike and Patsy had moved out
of the Hall just before the wedding, Angela still saw quite
a bit of Patsy as the couple were living at Blackwell
Manor till one of the farmhouses on the estate was ren-
ovated for them. Starr, thankfully, had decided that
farmhouse living was not for her, and had gone back to
California with Max, where she'd decided to stay... and
Angela, though she had never said so to anyone, hadn't
been sorry to see her go.

'I thought Aunt Patsy couldn't drive, Mummy.'

'I thought so too,' Angela said. 'Let's hurry and find
out what's going on!'

Patsy parked the car in the forecourt and jumped out
as they approached. 'I got my driving licence!' she cried.

'Well, I should hope so, since you're driving alone!'
Angela laughed breathlessly as she reached her friend.

'I sat the test this morning——'

'You didn't even tell me you were taking lessons!' Angela pretended to pout. 'And you call yourself a friend.'

'I wanted to surprise you!' Patsy looked up with a rueful grimace as large drops of rain started spattering on the roof of her car. 'Lordy, it's raining again—more like sleet than rain, actually! Let's go in—I'm dying for a cup of coffee.' She chuckled as they started towards the front door. 'Mike had the new Volvo delivered while I was sitting my test. A surprise. He was absolutely sure I would pass.'

Laughing happily, they all hurried up the steps. Once inside, as they were taking off their coats and boots, Patsy said to Nicky, 'I've brought something for you, love.'

'What is it, Aunt Patsy?'

'Remember we were talking about christenings the other day, and you told me you'd been christened but you didn't remember anything about it because you were a baby? Well, I brought the tape of your cousin's christening, so you can see exactly how it's done.'

'Oh, goody! May I be the one to put it in the VCR?'

Patsy looked questioningly at Angela.

'Oh, sure,' Angela said. 'He knows how to do it.'

Delving into her roomy bag, Patsy brought out the tape. 'Here you are, then, Nicky. You never did see it, Angela—would you like to watch it too?'

'Mmm. Let's use the TV in the library. Nicky, will you run to the kitchen and ask Nelly to bring us some coffee?'

Nicky kicked a red and yellow ball that was lying in the hallway, and followed it as it rolled towards the kitchen, but a few moments later, as Angela was ushering Patsy into the library, the ball came flying back across the hall, closely followed by Nicky.

'Nelly isn't in the kitchen, Mummy.'

'I've seen the tape half a dozen times already,' Patsy said, 'so why don't you two go ahead and watch it? I'll make the coffee. OK?'

'All right, Patsy. Thanks.'

Max had made a fine job of taping the christening, but as Angela and Nicky watched the ceremony each time there was a shot of Dominic she felt a familiar dull pain in the region of her heart. Though she had sworn she would never let herself care about him again, she knew, deep down inside, that she still loved him and always would. She knew he would have to come home soon—he just couldn't stay away forever—though Mike was at present managing the estate for him...and when he came back, what then? What kind of torture would it be, living in the same house, aching shamefully for his touch, yet knowing he despised her?

'Here I am, love—two coffees coming up!'

Angela welcomed Patsy's cheery voice, and was thankful to have her unhappy thoughts of Dominic interrupted. Nicky got up from the couch and was halfway across to the TV to switch off the tape and rewind it when Angela noticed that Patsy was looking for a place to lay down the tray.

'Darling,' she said to her son, 'before you do that, would you clear a place on the coffee-table for Patsy?' She herself crossed to the fire and gave the logs a poke, watching for a moment as sparks crackled up the chimney.

Patsy poured the coffee and then sat down by the fire. 'Well, Nicky, how did you enjoy the christening?'

Nicky had wandered to the middle of the room and was staring engrossedly at the TV screen. He didn't respond to Patsy's question.

'Darling, pay attention,' Angela said softly.

But Nicky didn't turn round. Still gazing raptly at the TV picture, he cried in an excited voice, 'It's you, Mummy, you and Uncle Mike! You're in a movie!'

Angela glanced in surprise at the TV, and her lips curved in a rueful smile as she saw herself and Mike tangled up together on a long sofa. 'Oh, dear...'

'Oh, dear, indeed!' Patsy's laughter was spontaneous and hearty. 'I'd forgotten that thing was still on tape!'

Angela chuckled. '*Love's Dark Shadow*. What fun we had that day—do you remember, Patsy?'

'I'll never forget—I don't think I've laughed so much in my whole life as I did——'

'Why is Uncle Mike kissing you, Mummy?' Nicky's smooth brow creased in a small frown.

'Try to explain your way out of *that*!' Patsy murmured *sotto voce*.

Angela grimaced. How *did* one explain that to a four-year-old? 'Starr used to be in movies, Nicky. One of the films she made was called *Love's Dark Shadow*, and she had kept a copy of the script—the...story. It happened to be lying around one afternoon, and Patsy saw it. She, your uncle Mike and I were having fun reading the different parts when Starr came home with a video camera she'd just bought. She told us we were doing it all wrong...and, in the end, she directed us as we acted out a scene for her, and she captured it on film.' Nodding towards the TV, Angela added, 'This is it.'

'Oh.' Once it had been explained, Nicky immediately lost interest. Wandering to the window, he looked out for a moment, and then said, 'Aunt Patsy, it's stopped raining. Can you take me for a spin in your new car?'

Patsy sipped the last of her coffee. 'Sure, Nicky——' she glanced at her watch '—but then I must dash. Want to come with us, Angie?'

Angela's gaze was fixed on the flickering image on the TV screen. 'You and Nicky go ahead—and if you're in a rush just drop him off at the door when you get back.' She shook her head as she watched Mike draw her into his arms. 'I'd forgotten this was so funny!' With an absent smile, she waved her hand. 'Bye, Patsy...and congrats on passing your test. Nicky, wear your warm jacket...'

As the door clicked shut behind them, Angela put down her mug and, curling her feet under her, sat back in the sofa. Wasn't laughter supposed to be the 'best medicine'? Perhaps watching this would help lift her from the doldrums. She hoped so; it was such an effort always trying to seem cheerful when there were others around.

With a sigh, she began resolutely concentrating all her attention on the scene being played out on the screen. The first part of the scene had been obliterated by the filming of the christening, but the latter part seemed to be here in its entirety... the part where the philandering protagonist, Harry, played by Mike, made love to Lulu, the scarlet woman, played by herself, on the eve of his wedding to the innocent Beth, played by Patsy. They had acted out the scene in the drawing-room, and had used the large sofa in place of the requisite bed. Now, as Angela watched, Mike was manoeuvring her across the room... towards the sofa.

'*Please leave now, darling. I'm feeling nervous to-night. If he should find out about us, there'll be——*'

'*Don't worry. He'll never find out. You've played every card right, and soon you'll have everything you want; you'll be able to look around as far as you can see and know the land all belongs to you.*'

'*Please go.*'

'*I will. But before I do... just one last kiss.*'

'*But one will lead to two, and two will lead to——*'

'*Two, my sweet, will lead to this.*'

Angela felt laughter bubbling up inside her as she watched. Mike, she recalled with a giggle, had hooked a foot around her ankles as he uttered the thickly passionate words and had toppled her on to the chesterfield with such force that it had knocked the breath from her lungs.

'*Oh...oh!*' Her gasp had literally been a gasp for air, but it sounded, on the videotape, like a gasp of raw desire.

That gasp marked the end of the scene, and at this point Patsy had choked out a strangled 'Cut!' before dissolving into uncontrollable hysterics. She and Mike had joined in, till they were literally rolling on the floor, Starr watching them with an air of cool amusement.

Now, stretching a little, Angela uncurled her legs from under her, and, running a hand through her hair, made to get up. But she had barely lifted herself from the cushion when she sensed she wasn't alone. Turning her head, she felt a shiver of shock as she saw a dark figure standing in the doorway.

It was Dominic. When had he come back?

As she stared numbly at him, she noticed, to her dismay, that his hands were clenched into fists by his sides, his face was pale as a November dawn, his eyes were dark and haunted.

He looked—the thought flashed out of nowhere into her bewildered mind—like a man who had been tortured.

But before she could speak, before she could even open her mouth to ask what was wrong, he posed a question of his own. And posed it in a voice of such unleashed anger that she felt a wave of apprehension sweep over her.

'Would you mind explaining,' he demanded in a voice of savage harshness, 'just what the *hell* that was all about?'

CHAPTER ELEVEN

'DOMINIC!' Angela slipped her feet on to the floor and stood up quickly. 'When did you get back...and what on earth's——?'

He slammed the door shut behind him with his fist with a blow of such terrifying force that Angela felt her heart give a jarring lurch...a lurch that was followed by a series of heavy, staggering heartbeats that threatened to block off her windpipe. Questions hammered at her brain as she saw the wild and hostile light in his eyes, but she couldn't utter them for the squeezing pain in her throat.

'Will you please explain what I saw...and heard...a moment ago?' His eyes burned into hers with fiery green menace as he began walking slowly towards her. 'You...and my half-brother...?'

He came to a stop three feet from her, and Angela tried to swallow back the agonising lump in her throat. Though she wanted to, she found she couldn't take her eyes from his; she was trapped, absolutely, in his hypnotic gaze.

Finally managing to clear her throat, she whispered in a thready voice, 'Patsy brought over the christening tape——' she twined her hands nervously before her '—and that——' biting her lip, she gestured with a brief nod of her head in the direction of the TV '—that was on it too——'

'And what, may I ask, was *that*?'

She could tell he was making a tremendous effort to appear controlled, yet the bulging tendons in his neck revealed a passion boiling just under the surface.

'That?' she asked, running the tip of her tongue over her suddenly parched lips. 'A video Starr took years

168

ago—Patsy and Mike and I were fooling around in the
drawing-room with an old script of hers, from a movie
called *Love's Dark Shadow*, and Starr filmed us——'

'She filmed you?' If Dominic's face had seemed drawn
before, now it seemed positively gaunt. Gaunt...and
ashen. 'You and Mike?' The accusation in his voice
chilled her blood. '*Making love*?'

Angela found herself stepping back, involuntarily...and she gave a defensive laugh. 'What are you
getting at? We were play-acting—if you'd seen the earlier
part——'

'Did you and Mike rehearse the scene——?'

'Of course not! I told you, we were fooling around in
the drawing-r——'

'And you never rehearsed the scene? Upstairs? In the
bedroom?'

'The *bedroom*?' Angela's sense of confusion increased. 'I'm sorry.' She crossed her arms over her breasts
and distractedly rubbed her hands up and down over her
upper arms. 'I've lost you...I can't seem to understand
what you're trying to say.'

Dominic began pacing up and down the room, his
breathing deep and ragged, and, as Angela stared at him,
she found a monstrous possibility thrusting its way into
her mind. Surely...*surely*...Dominic couldn't be
thinking, couldn't be implying...

Though she hadn't intended to, she found herself
speaking the words aloud, disbelievingly. 'You're
not...suggesting that Mike and I were...doing anything but...acting?' With her breath caught in her throat,
Angela waited numbly for his answer.

He stopped pacing and stood where he was, his back
to her, for a moment that to Angela seemed endless.
Finally, when she was about to *demand* a reply to her
question, he wheeled round and faced her again. Every
line on his face, every groove, seemed to have deepened—and, for the first time since she'd known him, he

looked every day his age. 'When did Starr make the tape?' he asked in a voice she barely recognised.

'It was the day before Patsy's wedding,' Angela said, with a flick of her head that was slightly defiant. 'Starr had bought the camera so the ceremony could be taped. She'd invited me to stay at the Hall because there wasn't room for me at Patsy's—you missed all the fun because you didn't get home till the morning of the wedding.'

'The fun.' With a suddenness that startled Angela, Dominic exhaled with a shuddering sound, and as he did so he bent his head, and rubbed the fingers of one hand roughly, savagely across his brow. When he looked up again, his face had a ravaged look. 'So what I overheard in your bedroom, when I went to your suite on the eve of the wedding, wasn't you and Mike making love...it was just voices on that tape...'

'On the eve of the wedding...? But...you weren't at the Hall then—you didn't arrive till the next day...'

Dominic slowly shook his head. 'No, you're wrong. If only you were right...how much better it would have been...'

'Dominic——' Angela straightened her back and looked him straight in the eye '—will you stop talking in riddles? I don't understand. You say you came home the night before the wedding...and you...overheard what you thought was Mike and myself making love...' Angela's voice trailed away as the full implication of what she was saying dawned on her with the impact of a blow in the stomach. 'You heard the tape...and you thought I was in bed with *Mike*? You thought I was capable of that kind of deception...that I was that kind of girl?'

'So Nick...really is...*my* son? But he's so fair——'

He broke off as he heard her gasp of horror.

'You thought Nicky was *Mike's* child?' Angela felt the beginnings of a hysterical laugh building inside her but somehow she managed to force it back; what was being enacted now between herself and Dominic was even more melodramatic, more farcical than the scene she had acted out on the tape with Mike. 'How *could* you?' she demanded in a thunderstruck tone. 'How could you ever have *imagined* that I'd do that? And with Mike, of all people. You thought I was having an affair with the husband of my best friend? That I could face Patsy afterwards—even be godmother to their son?' Angela shrank back from him as if she could no longer bear to be near him.

'Listen to me, Angela.' Dominic's voice was passionate, intense. 'You must try to understand——'

'Oh, my God,' Angela breathed, no longer listening to him but listening instead to her own brain, which was coming up with horrifying answers to the questions swirling around in her head. 'You thought I was just pretending Nicky was yours so that you could inherit the Hall? And you went along with that? You went along with it just so you could have what you always wanted— Hadleigh Estate? And you thought that was what *I'd* always wanted—to become mistress of Hadleigh Hall? Oh, Dominic——' there was a sobbing despair in her voice '—what kind of a man are you? How could you have believed I'd betray you... and my best friend... in such a way?'

'Haven't you ever heard of circumstantial evidence? I arrived in the middle of the night—I'd phoned Starr from Heathrow when I arrived, to let her know I was back, and she told me you were sleeping at the Hall. She told me she had put you in the Hyacinth Suite. I asked her not to let you know I'd be back early, I was going to surprise you. But it was you who surprised me. Why in God's name were you playing that tape at that time of the——?'

'I wasn't in the Hyacinth Suite, Dominic.' Angela's voice trembled. 'Starr changed her mind at the last minute and moved my things to the Daffodil Suite.'

'Then who was in the suite, who was playing the——?'

'It must have been Starr—no one else had any motivation to break us up. It was a set-up. She could see the way things were between us, and she wanted to make sure Mike and Patsy would have the first Elliott grandson.' Angela smiled bitterly. 'She's not all bad, though—she did try to get us together again, once it was safe to do so, once she had the grandchild she wanted.' '*You win*'. At last Angela thought she understood Starr's whispered words on the day of the christening.

Dominic was speaking, angrily, something about confronting Starr, but Angela interrupted wearily, 'Forget it—it doesn't really matter. And what good would it do? The fact that we've found out she was the cause of all our problems doesn't change anything. It doesn't change the fact that all this time you've believed me to be a conniving little tramp. It doesn't change the fact that even when you made your wedding vows you believed me to be a conniving little tramp; that, when you made love to me on our wedding night, you believed me to be a conniving little tramp.' She turned from him and started walking blindly towards the door.

'*Wait*, Angela, we have to talk——'

'We've nothing to talk about, Dominic. Trust and respect are the basis of any marriage—if a couple don't have those, they have nothing.' Ignoring his outstretched hand, she walked the last steps to the door—steadily, despite feeling as if her legs were going to give way at any moment. She could feel the tears begin to burn in her eyes and she had to get away before Dominic could see them. Opening the door quickly, she pushed it shut behind her.

As she stumbled towards the stairs, she heard a car door slamming outside. That would be Patsy, she thought distractedly, back with Nicky. Changing direction, she ran blindly to the front door, and jerked it open. Nicky was standing at the foot of the steps, in his quilted jacket, waving to Patsy as she began to pull away in her new Volvo.

'Wait!' Angela cried, signalling wildly to Patsy. Then she ran back into the hall, snatched up her handbag from the table by the phone, and grabbed her winter jacket from the closet. And she was just whirling around to make for the door again when she heard a sound behind her. Turning abruptly, she saw Dominic. He had come out of the drawing-room, and was standing looking at her, his green eyes anguished.

'Are you leaving?' His voice was thick with emotion.

'What is there to stay for?'

'We *have* to talk——'

'Talk?' she repeated in a tone of incredulity. 'You think I want to talk with you? The time for talking is past. The time for talking was when you overheard the tape. Didn't you have any guts, Dominic? Why didn't you storm into the bedroom if you believed Mike and I were having an affair? If you'd really loved me, as you claim to have done, why did you act like a...like a *wimp*? Did you just walk away, feeling sorry for yourself? Were you afraid of Mike, afraid you wouldn't be a match for him if it came to a fist fight? Surely a man who was any kind of a man would have done *something*...as a matter of...*honour*, if nothing else...instead of...instead of...'

Choking with tears, Angela ran towards the door. On the step outside, she found Nicky waiting, and, grasping his hand, pulled him to the car and bundled him into the back seat, before getting into the passenger seat beside an obviously stunned and bewildered Patsy.

'Don't ask me any questions,' Angela begged through her tears. 'Just...*please*...take me to the station.'

Controlling her concern and her natural curiosity with an obvious effort, Patsy swung the car away from the steps and along the drive. Angela didn't look back. Was Dominic standing on the top step, watching her leave? She didn't know. She didn't care...

With a blurred glance at her watch, she saw that if Patsy drove quickly they would just make the afternoon train south. 'Can you go a bit faster?' she pleaded. 'I don't want to miss the train.'

'Where are we going, Mummy?' Nicky's voice came plaintively from the back seat.

Angela sensed Patsy's eyes on her as she answered in a tight voice, 'We're going to Grandpa's for a little holiday, darling.'

'Will we be coming back to the Hall?'

'We'll talk about that later.'

'Oh, Angela, what's wrong?' Patsy's voice was filled with distress.

'Dominic and I have had a . . . fight,' Angela said, her voice low, so that Nicky wouldn't hear, and choked with tears. 'I . . . don't want to talk about it just now . . . if you don't mind. Sorry . . .'

'Oh, God . . .' Patsy's tone was tearful too, now, and bleak, but, to Angela's great relief, she refrained from asking the questions that must have been milling around in her head. And during the rest of the drive to the station she didn't say a word, but Angela could sense her concern, could sense that her old friend was desperately wishing she could comfort her in some way.

But of course she couldn't. There was no comfort to be obtained, from any source. The pain she'd felt five years ago when Dominic had jilted her was as nothing compared to the anguish tearing at her now. To have had a taste of heaven, and then to have it torn from her so cruelly, was more than she could bear.

When Patsy drove into the car park at the small station, Angela felt a stab of alarm as she saw that the train was already pulling in.

'We'll have to get our tickets on the train,' she cried, snatching open her car door almost before the vehicle had stopped. 'It only stops here for a minute.' Quickly, she tore open the rear door, and dragged Nicky out. 'Take my hand,' she urged, 'and run as fast as you can.'

Patsy ran ahead to the nearest coach, and, wrenching the door open, helped Angela hoist Nicky aboard.

Immediately, he scrambled to the other side of the coach and hopped on to one of the cushioned seats.

Patsy jumped back on to the platform and as she did Angela crashed the door shut. After a moment's struggling, she managed to push down the window, and, grasping the lower part of the frame, looked down at her friend.

'Thanks awfully, Patsy.' Her words came out chokingly. 'I . . . I feel dreadful, asking you to drive your car in such a rush, when you've only just passed your——'

'He won't come after you, you know.' Patsy's face was pale, her eyes great blue pools of sorrow. 'He won't chase after you and beg you to come back. Never. Not after what happened with his mother when——'

The shriek of the train whistle drowned out the rest of Patsy's words. Angela knew she was still speaking— her lips were moving . . . but the train was pulling away along the platform, and though Angela craned her head out the window, and called back in an urgent voice, 'What did you say, Patsy, about Dominic's mother?' it was too late. Though Patsy ran alongside the train for a bit, shouting after them, her cries were lost, the engine gathering speed very quickly, and within seconds they were out of earshot.

The last thing Angela saw before the train curved round the bend at the end of the long platform was Patsy, standing like a lost soul with her arms clutched around her waist, and fluffy snowflakes beginning to fall gently around her.

The first snow of the year, Angela thought sadly as she pulled the window shut again. Usually the beautiful sight lifted her heart, but not today.

She had already known Dominic wouldn't chase after her. He wasn't that kind of a man. He would never plead, never beg. But what was it Patsy had started to say, as the train whistle cut her off? '*He won't chase after you . . .*

Never. Not after what happened with his mother when——'

When what? What had she been referring to?

Well, Angela reflected unhappily as she sank into the seat beside Nicky, she would never know now what it was. And it really didn't make any difference, did it? She didn't *want* Dominic chasing after her; she didn't want anything more to do with a man who could think the dreadful things Dominic had thought about her.

She bent her head and felt warm tears fall on her hands, clenched in her lap. It's over, she whispered to herself, it's over.

And this time, she knew, it was for good.

It was dark by the time the train reached Brockton. The snow must have started there much earlier, because the station platform was already thickly carpeted.

Nicky was in a disgruntled mood, and as they walked past the brightly lit cafeteria next to the waiting-room he said, 'I'm hungry. I want something to eat, Mummy. Can't we have something here, before we walk to Grandpa's?'

It might be a good idea, Angela thought with a tired sigh. No use turning up at Hawthorne Cottage with a cranky child. 'All right,' she said, making an effort to sound upbeat. 'I could do with a cup of coffee myself.'

The cafeteria was poorly heated and cheerless, the waitress overweight and surly-looking.

'Could we have one small coffee, and a cup of hot chocolate, please?' Angela asked.

'One coffee, one hot chocolate—anything else?' the waitress snapped.

Nicky pointed to a display of pie slices. 'May I have some lemon pie?' he asked, looking up at Angela.

'Mmm. One serving of lemon pie, and one of cherry,' she said to the waitress.

'Yuk, cherry!' Nicky screwed up his face.

'Humph!' The waitress glared at him as she scooped out the desserts and thumped them on the counter-top. 'Kids nowadays—in my day they were seen and not heard. And that's as how it should be, in my opinion!'

Biting back a sarcastic retort, Angela paid her bill and, placing everything on a tray, led Nicky over to a small Formica-topped table by one of the windows.

'Sip carefully—make sure it isn't too hot,' she warned him as he cupped his small hands round the heavy stoneware mug. Her own coffee was bitter, and she ladled sugar into it in an attempt to make it more palatable.

'He'll never chase after you... Never. Not after what happened with his mother when——'

Despite her efforts not to think about Dominic, Angela found Patsy's words returning to her... as they had, several times, on the train journey. What had her old friend been trying to say, when the whistle had drowned her out?

Oh, it really didn't make any difference, she thought dully, not to *anything*.

But still...

Making an impulsive decision, she pushed back her chair and got to her feet. 'Nicky,' she said, 'I have to call Aunt Patsy. I'm going to see if I can find a phone.'

'All right, Mummy.' He looked at her over the rim of his mug. 'There's one over there.' He pointed behind her.

Angela glanced round and saw the phone just inside the door. 'So there is, you clever boy.'

She got through to Patsy right away.

'It's me—Angela.'

'Angela! Are you calling from Brockton?'

'Mmm. Patsy——' she cleared her throat '—I'm curious... What were you trying to tell me at the station... something about Dominic's mother...? I couldn't hear, because of the whistle.'

There was a short pause at the other end, a pause which seemed awkward to Angela, and then Patsy said,

'Oh, dear...I had second thoughts about...I really shouldn't have said what I di—— '

'Patsy...please!'

She heard Patsy sigh. There was the longest silence, the only sounds Angela could hear being the clatter of dishes as the waitress cleared one of the tables. Chewing her lower lip, she was just thinking that Patsy was going to turn down her request for information when she heard her friend say, in a reluctant voice, 'It's just something Mummy told me years ago...and I'm sure she didn't want it repeated——'

'You know you can trust me, Patsy. Whatever you tell me won't go any further.'

'Oh, Angela... Oh, all right.' Patsy lowered her voice, as if to ensure her words wouldn't be overheard, as she went on, 'I'll tell you. It may help you to understand Dominic. You knew that his mother deserted his father and took off with another man when Dominic was just a child?'

'Yes, you told me about that when we were still in school. Dominic was eight at the time, I think you said.'

'That's right. Angela, what I didn't tell you is that...the day his mother took off...Dominic had a rather ghastly experience. The man—I don't know who he was—had come to pick her up, and the two of them were upstairs in the master bedroom at the Hall, making love, and Dominic...'

Angela frowned as Patsy hesitated. 'You mean...he heard them——'

'He not only heard them...he saw them. Apparently he'd been on an outing with some schoolfriend and had been dropped off at home earlier than expected, and he'd gone upstairs to look for his mother. He heard her voice...and a man's voice...and when he went into the bedroom, thinking she was there with Dom...he found her...in bed...stark naked with a man he'd never seen before.'

'Oh, my God——'

'Exactly.' Patsy's voice was hard. 'The poor kid. But what happened after was even worse. His mother had already packed her bags, so she and her lover—after they got dressed, of course!—went out to the man's car…and Dominic ran after them, begging his mother not to go. He clutched at her skirt and tried to stop her, but she paid him no attention, just tore herself away from him…and then when he tried to climb on to the car as it was pulling away, and hung on to the open window, she grabbed his little hands and prised them free, and pushed him back and he fell down on to the drive——'

'Patsy!'

'—and they didn't stop. They left him there, bruised and sore, sobbing his heart out. He was still lying there, limp and still, when Dom came up from the stables an hour or so later. He was quite ill, Mummy said, for a long time after. She and Dom had always been great friends, and he told her everything that had happened. Dominic was actually delirious, and he'd rambled on and on, and his father eventually pieced the whole thing together.'

Angela hadn't realised she was crying till she saw that the picture on the wall in front of her was a vague blur. Distraughtly, she dragged a hand over her eyes, and tried to swallow the lump painfully blocking her throat.

'Are you still there, love?' Patsy's anxiety was obvious in her tone.

'Mmm. And now I know,' Angela's voice was shaky and filled with despair, 'why you were so sure Dominic would never chase after me…why he would never chase after any woman. Never beg any woman to come back.'

There was a sniffling sound at the other end of the line. 'I'm sorry, Angela. I'm so sorry that things have turned out this way.'

'So am I.' Angela's voice was a mere whisper. 'So am I.' Unable to say another word, she hung up the phone.

Back at the table with Nicky, she mechanically picked up her mug of now lukewarm coffee. She could feel a hollow rumbling in her stomach but, though she hadn't eaten for hours, she didn't feel at all hungry. She hadn't even started the cherry pie but she had no appetite for it.

Still, she had paid for it, and it wouldn't be a good example to Nicky to leave it. She should take a bite or two...

She did, and wished she hadn't. The pastry tasted like cardboard.

'Did you talk to Aunt Patsy?' Nicky asked.

'Mmm.'

'What were you talking about?'

'Oh, this and that.' She forced a smile and then lightly changed the subject. 'How's your pie?'

'Yummy. How's yours?'

'It's fine.' She ate another spoonful, but it seemed to stick in her throat. Only with the greatest difficulty did she manage to swallow it. Putting down her fork, she patted her lips with her paper napkin, and as she did she saw Nicky grimace. 'What's wrong?' she asked.

He gave a little shudder. 'I'm *never* going to get married,' he responded forcefully.

Startled, Angela stared at him in dismay. What had brought *that* on? she wondered. Surely he hadn't overheard her conversation just now with Patsy? Or had he, more likely, overheard her in the car, telling Patsy she and Dominic had had a fight? That, of course, was the very last thing she wanted, for Nicky to get hurt. She would have to talk with him, coax out of his little mind just what he was thinking... and then, somehow, reassure him.

With an attempt at nonchalance, she laid her mug on the table and said lightly, 'Why not, Nicky?'

'Because I just *hate* cherry pie.'

Angela looked at him in puzzlement. She knew he hated cherry pie—it was one of the few things he disliked. But what on earth did that have to do with getting married?

'You think... that if you're married you'll have to eat *cherry pie*?'

Nicky swallowed the piece of lemon pie in his mouth before answering. 'Mmm. I heard you promise Daddy, on your wedding-day, in the chapel.'

Angela looked bewilderedly at him. 'Promise what, darling?'

'Promise to love cherries,' he said impatiently. 'You promised him you'd love cherries and obey. Yuk, I hate cherries. I'll never get married.'

'*To love, cherish, and obey* ...'

Angela felt as if someone had taken her heart and squeezed it so tightly that it was bleeding. 'Oh, Nicky,' she murmured, a catch in her voice, 'darling—that's not what I said—to love cherries and obey. What I said was...''to love, cherish and obey.'' *Cherish*.'

'Oh.' Nicky clasped his hands around his mug again and looked at her seriously. 'What's...''cherish''?'

Angela swallowed hard. '''Cherish'' is to keep something...or someone...safe. Someone who is dear to you. And to take care of them if anything does go wrong— if you fall down and hurt yourself, I hold you, and hug you, and kiss you, and make you feel better.'

'So if Daddy falls down, and hurts himself, you'll cherish him. You'll hold him, and hug him, and kiss him, and make him feel better.'

Angela found it almost impossible to speak for the emotion tightening her throat. 'Yes.' Her voice was husky.

'That was a promise.' Nicky was matter-of-fact. 'And promises are important, aren't they, Mummy? You've always told me so.'

Now that he had the matter settled in his own mind— the matter of cherry pie and marriage—he stopped talking and concentrated on his hot chocolate.

Angela sank back in her seat, feeling as if all the life had been drained out of her body. Nicky's words had struck like a lance at her heart. All those promises she'd made—to love, to cherish, the promises she'd assured Dominic would be forever—she'd run out on them all, at the first sign of trouble.

Forcing herself to face the facts—unpleasant though those facts were—she had to admit, with a great feeling of shame, that ever since finding out how Dominic had misjudged her she had been positively wallowing in self-pity and feelings of self-righteousness.

What meanness of spirit had made her walk out on him without letting him try to explain? Would he have told her, today, about his mother, if she had stayed and listened? Every instinct told her he would. But she hadn't given him that chance.

She felt her heart ache for Dominic, the boy, who had stumbled in on his mother and her lover. No wonder Dominic, the man, had reacted the way he had when he'd overheard the tape of herself and Mike. Had he felt a hideous sense of *déjà vu*? *This*, he would have said to himself in horror, *has happened before* . . .

But the first time, he had walked right into it.

And the consequences had been so traumatic for a child that the effect on him would be everlasting.

Then it had happened a second time, and the voices in the bedroom would have reopened wounds in his heart, exposing him once again to memories he'd probably tried to suppress for many years. Memories from hell. Memories of betrayal, memories of rejection, memories of despair, memories of injury, mental and physical.

No wonder he had chosen not to expose himself to that experience again. No wonder he had chosen to harness his self-control; no wonder he'd chosen, like a wounded tiger, to go to his lair and lick his wounds in solitude. Only a fool dived into the same hell-hole twice . . .

He had asked her to stay. Asked her to stay and talk. But he hadn't *begged* her . . . and she knew now this man would never beg—*and she knew why not.* But he *had* asked. And instead of agreeing to do so, instead of listening to what he had to say, she too had rejected him. In this, she was probably worse than his mother. Perhaps his mother had never told him she loved him, whereas she . . .

Remorse flooded through her, and she brushed a tear from her cheek with the back of her hand. Why had she acted liked a child, instead of the mature adult she was supposed to be? Why hadn't she agreed to sit down with Dominic and talk out their problems? Why had she run away from them? Surely it was she, and not Dominic, who lacked courage——

'Mummy!' Nicky was looking at her with panic in his eyes. 'We forgot about Maggie—she's in my bedroom! I can't go to Grandpa's; I can't go to sleep without Maggie. And she won't be able to go to sleep without me. She'll cry all night.' Nicky's face crumpled. 'I won't be there to . . . comfort her.'

As he dissolved into gulping sobs, Angela drew in a deep breath. Perhaps it wasn't too late. Yes, she had hurled some dreadful accusations at Dominic when she'd lashed out at him . . . horrid, hurtful accusations. But she hadn't been in possession of all the facts. If she went back, and told him she was ready to talk, would he forgive her for deserting him? If she didn't try, she would never forgive herself.

Getting up quickly, she lifted her handbag, and rounded the table to where Nicky was bent over the table, weeping. 'It's all right, darling,' she murmured, 'don't cry.' She crouched down, and, wiping his tear-stained cheeks, went on, 'We're going back—I have to talk with your father.'

Outside, a strong wind had risen, and it was splattering against the walls of the station buildings. It was not a night to be out. But a few minutes later they were on their way back towards the exit, Nicky with a lighter heart, and Angela with two tickets to Hadleigh tucked in her purse.

'When's the next train, Mummy?'

'In an hour. We'll have time to walk to Grandpa's and say hello before coming back to catch it. We'll phone Daddy from Grandpa's, and ask him to meet us at Hadleigh station.'

With their heads bent against the wind, they exited the station and waited at the side of the road for a car to pass before crossing. It was a black BMW, the same model as Dominic's, and Angela felt her heart lurch nervously. A few hours from now, she and Nicky would be climbing into just such a car, with Dominic at the wheel. What would be the outcome of their trip?

The car braked loudly, and swerved to a stop just inches from where Angela stood on the edge of the pavement. 'Some people just don't know how to drive!' she gasped in outrage as she jerked Nicky back.

But even as she stood there, glaring angrily in the direction of the driver's seat, the car door flew open and a tall figure shot out. Slamming the door shut, he walked swiftly around the bonnet...towards them. For a moment, Angela could do nothing but stare in disbelief. It was Dominic. Black hair dishevelled, features taut, he was still wearing what he'd had on earlier—the white shirt, the striped tie, the dark trousers.

But no jacket. No coat. He was going to catch pneumonia, Angela found herself thinking in some distant, disembodied part of her mind.

But he had come after her.

She felt as if her veins were suddenly bubbling with champagne. He loved her still, and, despite the cruel things she'd said to him, he still wanted her. Oh, it was truly a miracle!

'It's Daddy!' Nicky hopped up and down excitedly. 'And look what he's brought!'

In Dominic's arms was Maggie. And as Angela gazed blankly at the threadbare bulldog she felt her heart contract. Dominic hadn't come after her. He had followed them only to give Nicky his toy, knowing how lost the child would be without Maggie.

He didn't look at her as he stopped in front of them.

'You forgot something,' he said to Nicky. Crouching down, he handed the bulldog to his son. 'Here you are, Nick, I knew you wouldn't be able to sleep without her.' He put his arms around the sturdy little body, and buried his face in the child's neck. It was the first time, Angela realised with an aching heart, that he'd had the opportunity to hug Nicky since discovering this was really his own son. Finally, with a bone-weary sigh, he released the boy and straightened.

'Thanks, Daddy.' Nicky grinned up at him cheerfully. 'We were on our way to Grandpa's for a holiday but we——'

'You're on your way back to your father's?' At last, Dominic turned to Angela. Snowflakes were already thick on his hair…and clustered on his eyelashes, making his expression unreadable. 'Would you like a drive?'

Not wanting to speak in case he heard the misery in her voice, Angela could only shake her head. '*He won't chase after you… Never. Not after what happened with his mother——*'

And he hadn't chased after her. Perhaps he hadn't loved her after all. Or perhaps he was too proud to tell her. Too proud. Too afraid. Too afraid to risk another rejection.

But she did love him. And she wasn't too proud, she wasn't too afraid. At least, if she was, she wasn't going to show it, and she wasn't going to let it stop her. She'd go down on her hands and knees in the snow, if she had to, and ask him to take her back. She knew, if she wanted him, she would have to be the one to make that first move.

Wordlessly, she fumbled in her handbag for the two tickets to Hadleigh. She would show them to him, show him she had changed her mind and had been planning to return.

'Dominic.' She finally found the tickets, and, curling her fingers around them, extricated them from her purse. 'Will you——?'

She didn't get a chance to finish her question. With a sudden move that took her breath away, Dominic grasped her by the shoulders. 'Angela,' his voice was thick with pain, 'I want you to come home.' He shook his head vehemently as she opened her mouth to speak. 'Just listen...please. When you walked away from me this afternoon, I felt as if I was stumbling about in a cold, dark world—I never want to feel that way again. I know I've said and done a lot of things that have hurt you, but if you love me as much as I love you—as much as I've always loved you—then I know you'll forgive me.' She could now see past the snowflakes clustered on his lashes, could see the stark agony in his green eyes. 'I can't live without you, Angela. And if I hadn't found you here tonight I'd have followed you to the ends of the earth, for a world without you is not a place I want to be. Oh, God, Angie, just say...please say...you'll come home with me. If you want me to, I'll go down on my hands and knees——'

Angela felt an exquisite ache in her heart, an ache that was a combination of tenderness, love...and soaring joy. 'Oh, Dominic, darling, you need never go down on your hands and knees to me.' Her eyes glistened with tears as she held out the tickets. 'Will you do me a favour?' she asked, her voice breaking. 'I just bought these. Two tickets home. We were coming back to you on the very next train. Could you return them? I won't need them now——'

As she spoke, an extra strong gust of wind caught the two tickets and whisked them away into the sky among the swirling snowflakes. She gasped in dismay. 'Oh, Dominic——'

'Let them go.' With a smothered groan, he drew her to him. One of his hands, firm and masterful, was tangled in her hair, the other cupped her head. 'Two train tickets,' he whispered in her ear. 'That's a small price to pay for knowing you were coming back to me.'

'Oh, Dominic.' She clung to him, desperately, feeling the warmth of his body through the snow-damp fabric of his shirt. 'I love you so much.'

After a long moment, he said quietly, 'There's one thing I don't understand, Angela. When I warned you five years ago never to come back to the Hall, you and Mike weren't having an affair, so why in God's name did you think I acted the way I did?'

'I . . . thought you didn't want me because . . . I'd given in to you, that night by the lake.'

'You thought. . . Oh, dear God——' his grip tightened and she felt him tremble '—you couldn't have been more wrong. That night by the lake is my most cherished memory.'

'Daddy. . .'

Dominic claimed Angela's lips in a worshipping, lingering kiss before he bent down to scoop Nicky up into their circle of love. 'Yes, son.' He brushed the snow gently from Nicky's hair. 'What is it?'

'Are you and Mummy going to love and cherish each other forever?'

Dominic and Angela looked at each other, over their son's blond head, and when she saw the steady, unquenchable flame of love in Dominic's eyes Angela felt as if her heart was dancing like the snowflakes swirling around them.

'Yes,' they answered together, 'forever and ever.'

'And *that*,' Nicky whispered to Maggie, whose one eye winked up at him brightly, 'is a promise.'

MILLS & BOON

EXCITING NEW COVERS

To reflect the ever-changing contemporary romance series
we've designed new covers which perfectly capture the
warmth, glamour and sophistication of modern-day romantic
situations.

We know, because we've designed them with your comments
in mind, that you'll just love the bright, warm, romantic
colours and the up-to-date new look.

WATCH OUT FOR THESE NEW COVERS

From October 1993   Price £1.80

Proudly present to you...

BETTY NEELS' 100TH ROMANCE

Betty has been writing for Mills & Boon Romances for over 20 years. She began once she had retired from her job as a Ward Sister. She is married to a Dutchman and spent many years in Holland. Both her experiences as a nurse and her knowledge and love of Holland feature in many of her novels.

Her latest romance *'AT ODDS WITH LOVE'* is available from August 1993, price £1.80.

EXPERIENCE THE EXOTIC

VISIT . . . INDONESIA, TUNISIA, EGYPT AND MEXICO . . . THIS SUMMER

Enjoy the experience of exotic countries
with our Holiday Romance Pack

Four exciting new romances by favourite
Mills & Boon authors.

Available from July 1993   Price: £7.20

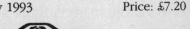

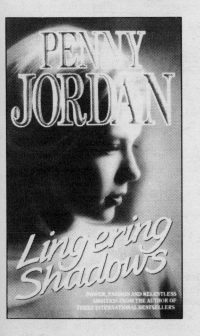

Next Month's Romances

Each month you can choose from a wide variety of romance with Mills & Boon. Below are the new titles to look out for next month, why not ask either Mills & Boon Reader Service or your Newsagent to reserve you a copy of the titles you want to buy – just tick the titles you would like and either post to Reader Service or take it to any Newsagent and ask them to order your books.

Please save me the following titles:	Please tick	√
SIMPLY IRRESISTIBLE	Miranda Lee	
HUNTER'S MOON	Carole Mortimer	
AT ODDS WITH LOVE	Betty Neels	
A DANGEROUS MAGIC	Patricia Wilson	
TOWER OF SHADOWS	Sara Craven	
THE UNMARRIED BRIDE	Emma Goldrick	
SWEET BETRAYAL	Helen Brooks	
COUNTERFEIT LOVE	Stephanie Howard	
A TEMPORARY AFFAIR	Kate Proctor	
SHADES OF SIN	Sara Wood	
RUTHLESS STRANGER	Margaret Mayo	
BITTERSWEET LOVE	Cathy Williams	
CAPTIVE BRIDE	Rosemary Carter	
WILLING OR NOT	Liza Hadley	
MASTER OF NAMANGILLA	Mons Daveson	
LOVE YOUR ENEMY	Ellen James	
A FOOLISH HEART	Laura Martin	

If you would like to order these books in addition to your regular subscription from Mills & Boon Reader Service please send £1.80 per title to: Mills & Boon Reader Service, Freepost, P.O. Box 236, Croydon, Surrey, CR9 9EL, quote your Subscriber No:.................................... (If applicable) and complete the name and address details below. Alternatively, these books are available from many local Newsagents including W.H.Smith, J.Menzies, Martins and other paperback stockists from 13 August 1993.

Name:...

Address:..

....Post Code:.........................

To Retailer: If you would like to stock M&B books please contact your regular book/magazine wholesaler for details.

You may be mailed with offers from other reputable companies as a result of this application. If you would rather not take advantage of these opportunities please tick box ☐